Into the TALL, TALL Grass

Into the
TALL,
TALL
Grass

by Loriel Ryon

Margaret K. McElderry Books
New York London Toronto Sydney New Delhi

MARGARET K. McELDERRY BOOKS
An imprint of Simon & Schuster Children's Publishing Division
1230 Avenue of the Americas, New York, New York 10020
MARGARET K. McELDERRY BOOKS is a trademark of Simon & Schuster, Inc.
For information about special discounts for bulk purchases, please
contact Simon & Schuster Special Sales at 1-866-506-1949 or
business@simonandschuster.com.
The Simon & Schuster Speakers Bureau can bring authors to your
live event. For more information or to book an event, contact the
Simon & Schuster Speakers Bureau at 1-866-248-3049 or visit our
website at www.simonspeakers.com.
Jacket design by Debra Sfetsios-Conover
Interior design by Irene Metaxatos
The text for this book was set in Cormorant Garamond.
Manufactured in the United States of America
0220 FFG
First Edition
10 9 8 7 6 5 4 3 2 1
Library of Congress Cataloging-in-Publication Data
Names: Ryon, Loriel, author.
Title: Into the tall, tall grass / Loriel Ryon.
Description: First edition. | New York : Margaret K. McElderry Books, [2020] |
Audience: Ages 10 up. | Audience: Grades 7–9. | Summary: Yolanda sets out with
family and friends to help her grandmother and discovers long-buried secrets
about a family curse and the healing power of the magic surrounding her.
Identifiers: LCCN 2019032230 (print) | ISBN 9781534449671 (hardcover) |
ISBN 9781534449695 (eBook)
Subjects: CYAC: Magic—Fiction. | Ability—Fiction. | Secrets—Fiction. |
Sisters—Fiction. | Friendship—Fiction. | Grandmothers—Fiction.
Classification: LCC PZ7.1.R98 Int 2020 (print) | DDC [Fic]—dc23
LC record available at https://lccn.loc.gov/2019032230

For Quinn and London:
In becoming your mother,
I realized anything is possible.

For Greg: My rock, my teammate,
my partner, and my love.
Your unwavering support means
the world to me.

I love you.

One

YOLANDA crept to the bedroom door, cracking it just so and peering inside. Her *abuela*, Wela, was lying in bed with a yellow serape tucked beneath her arms, her chest barely rising. Three orange-and-black butterflies nestled into her long white curls, their wings opening and closing ever so slightly as the morning sun flickered through the tree branches outside the window. It was exactly the same sight it had been for the past two weeks.

Yolanda sighed in disappointment and pushed open the door, letting it groan loudly on its hinges, hoping the sound would cause Wela to stir. *Wake up. Wela, please wake up.* But Wela didn't move.

Was this all her fault? She sighed and walked over to the nightstand, twisting the vase of scarlet milkweed blossoms toward the light. Two butterflies sipped nectar from the wilting flowers. She brought the vase to Wela's fingertips in hopes that her touch would liven the blossoms. But they remained wilted, and she made a mental note to switch them out before she left for school.

The way the light danced across the serape and the fine lines surrounding Wela's closed pale lips made Yolanda's heart sink even lower. She'd seen this before, less than a year ago.

Dying.

It was too soon. She couldn't go through this again.

Wela had fallen into the sleep two weeks ago, and as many things were with Wela, it was a mystery. The doctors said there was no reason she shouldn't wake. Everything appeared normal on all the tests. Yolanda replayed her argument with her *abuela* over and over again, desperately hoping it wasn't all her fault. The sad look in Wela's eyes and the way she'd held out her arms for Yolanda haunted her. Why did Yolanda have to get so angry? Why couldn't she let it go? But when she thought of everything that was lost, she felt sick to her stomach.

Yolanda walked over to Wela's bookcase and ran her fingers along the textbook bindings. *Organic Chemistry. Cel-*

lular *Biology. Human Anatomy. Fundamental Entomology. Botany.* They were a mix of Wela's and Welo's textbooks. Wela had never gotten around to cleaning Welo's books out after he died. Next to the books there was a sapphire urn atop a black metal box with a tiny lock. Yolanda averted her eyes as the lump sat heavy in her throat. She couldn't even look at it without forcing back tears. Even though it had been nearly a year, she still couldn't bring herself to linger on her *abuelo*'s urn.

She moved to Wela's vanity and dug around in her wooden jewelry box until she found her favorite pair of earrings: silver double helices Wela had picked up at a science conference a few years ago. Wela certainly wouldn't mind her borrowing them for the big day. Yolanda looped them in her ears and shook her head in the mirror. Perfect. They glimmered against her wild chocolate curls and matched her DNA IS LIFE T-shirt. Her fingers brushed the cool stone of the bolo tie at her throat. She closed her eyes. The earrings for Wela, the tie for Welo.

A silver picture frame was lying facedown on the vanity. She picked it up and turned it over, her fingers lingering on the cool metal. Why was it facedown? Had it fallen over? It was a faded black-and-white photograph of three children in front of an enormous pecan tree. Two girls and a boy. The girls stood in front of the tree, their arms outstretched, holding a handful of pecans in each palm. The boy was hanging upside down from the lower branches, making a silly face.

She set the frame upright on the vanity, walked over to the side of the bed, and knelt. As the butterflies opened their delicate wings in Wela's hair, Yolanda's tears began to fall, for when she was alone was the only time she let her true feelings out.

"I'm so sorry, Wela. Just tell me how to fix this. How do I fix this?"

Yolanda buried her face in the clean serape, which smelled faintly like green apples.

"It's not your fault, *mija*."

Her head snapped up at Wela's voice. It couldn't be . . . could it? "Wela?"

Wela's eyes were closed and her chest gently rose with each sleeping breath. She didn't appear to be awake at all.

"I'm so sorry, Violeta," Wela whispered, her lips barely moving. *"Lo siento, mi hermana."*

Violeta? Yolanda sucked in her breath and her heart leapt. Wela was waking up. Yolanda leaned in, brushing a stray curl from Wela's forehead, desperately searching her face for any sign of consciousness. "Wela, it's me, Yolanda, *su nieta*. Your granddaughter. I'm right here." She placed a hand on Wela's wrinkled brown arm to calm her.

For a moment the butterflies in Wela's long white curls stopped pumping their wings, pausing midair and showing off their lacy patterns.

And Wela opened her eyes.

Two

YOLANDA gasped. "Wela!"

The bedroom door burst open, and Yosemite and Rosa-lind Franklin, their two French bulldogs, chased each other around the bed, barking and nipping at each other, their nails scraping against the wooden floor.

Drops of sweat rose on the back of Yolanda's neck as she jumped to her feet.

"What are you doing in here?" Sonja, her sister, leaned against the doorframe and took a large bite of a cold tamale.

"You scared me." Yolanda glanced at Wela, hoping that she was still awake, but her eyes were closed again. Her heart sank. She could swear Wela had just woken up. "Did you see that?" she asked.

"See what?" Sonja said through a mouthful of food.

Yolanda hung her head. "Nothing." She must have imagined it.

Rosalind Franklin, her little black dog with the flipped-up ears, popped out from underneath the bed with one of Wela's brown leather *chanclas* in her mouth.

"You better get that. She'll chew them up like she did to my brand-new hiking boots," Sonja said, pointing. Yosemite, Sonja's dog, pranced over to Sonja and rubbed her head against Sonja's leg.

"Oh, right, because there is no way it was your dog." Yolanda rolled her eyes and got down on all fours, though she knew in her heart Rosalind Franklin was definitely the guilty party. She pulled on Rosalind Franklin's collar, but her head slipped right out of it. It was purple, embroidered with her name and linked double helices, like DNA. Wela had it made when they first got the dogs. Yosemite's was embroidered with pine trees and her name. Yolanda stooped down again and tried to wiggle the shoe out of Rosalind Franklin's mouth. "Give it up, girl."

Her dog growled playfully and then wiggled her little black butt until she crashed into the bed, startling herself and letting the *chancla* go. Yolanda laughed. "Girl, you are such a—"

"Menace?" Sonja offered.

"No, she's a . . . delight. A breath of fresh air. She gets me," Yolanda said, snatching the other *chancla* off the floor and slapping both onto the vanity. "More than anyone else around here."

She walked over to her sister. "Aren't the tamales dry?"

"Not with ketchup." Sonja wiped a smudge of red from her lip and onto her shorts.

"Gross." Yolanda shook her head. "I can't believe you eat tamales with ketchup."

"Welo ate them like that."

Yolanda fake gagged and tried to push past Sonja, but instinctively ducked when she spotted the three bees flying around Sonja's auburn braids. Ugh, the bees. She couldn't escape them. They were always there, making her miserable.

"Mrs. Patel is here. She said she needs to talk to us," Sonja said.

"Can you move"—Yolanda stared at the bees—"them?"

Sonja straightened herself and walked toward the kitchen, her bees trailing behind.

The bees came on their twelfth birthday, a month after their *abuelo* died. It started with one, but by the end of the day, when Sonja was surrounded by bees darting in and out of her braids, Wela had declared that Sonja's gift was definitely the bees.

"*Las abejas*," she had said, hugging Sonja, her eyes shining with a mix of pride and sadness. "Just like my great-grandmother." Wela had pressed her palm to her chest. "*Mi bisabuela.*"

Yolanda waited the rest of the day, the following weeks, and then months for her gift to come.

But it never did.

It wasn't just that Sonja got the special family trait and Yolanda didn't that made them so different. Sonja looked like Dad—tall, thin, and pale, red-haired and freckled— whereas Yolanda favored Wela and Mamá's side of the family. Shorter, darker, and rounder, with an unruly mane of chocolate curls.

How they could be twins puzzled nearly everyone they met. *Twins? But you look nothing alike*, people would say. Sonja, the more patient one, would take a few moments to explain the difference between identical and fraternal twins, while Yolanda would roll her eyes, incredulous that people could be so uninformed about basic human repro- duction.

"Can't you leave the bees outside?" Yolanda again tried to push past her sister. "Isn't that why Wela got you the bee house in the first place?"

Sonja didn't move. She frowned and stuffed another bite of tamale in her mouth. "You know Wela doesn't like you snooping through Welo's things. She already got rid of most of his stuff."

"Do *not* bring that up to me," Yolanda snapped. She scolded herself for her tone, but she couldn't help it. The fact that all of Welo's notes were gone—she could hardly stand it. It was like no one even cared.

The bees flew around her sister's head like a crown of tiny beasts.

Buzzing, humming.

Taunting her.

Why, of all things, did it have to be bees?

Yolanda took a deep breath before she said something she would regret and followed Sonja into the kitchen.

Mrs. Patel, wearing a white lab coat over a pair of lavender scrubs, placed a Tupperware container in the refrigerator. "Good morning, girls! Are you ready for the science fair?"

The girls nodded.

Mrs. Patel brushed a hair from her face. She had changed the hoop she usually wore in her nose to a tiny gold stud. "I'm so sorry I didn't get to come by last night. I was at the hospital later than I thought. How is Josefa this morning?"

"The same," Yolanda said, shrugging. She must have imagined it. All of it, Wela's eyes opening, the whispering. "Still asleep."

Mrs. Patel nodded. "I'm afraid we have some big decisions to make. Since we can't get in touch with your dad, things are getting quite complicated." Mrs. Patel tapped her index finger to her lips, jingling the gold bracelets on her wrist. "I've spoken with the military and they won't tell me anything. His mission could take months. We need to find an alternative situation for you girls, and so . . . a social worker will be coming by this afternoon."

Yolanda and her sister erupted at the same time.

"You don't think Wela is going to wake up from this?" Sonja asked.

"A social worker?" Yolanda ran her fingers through her hair. This was a disaster. She knew exactly what this meant. "They're going to send us to foster care!"

"No one is saying you'll have to do that." Mrs. Patel raised her hands defensively. "Josefa could still wake up. But in the meantime, we can't have you living here all alone with her. Because I live up the road, we could get away with it for a few days, but now things are starting to become more serious. And with us leaving soon . . ." Her voice trailed off. "Without a will, I'm guessing as to what she would want me to do."

"A will?" Yolanda didn't like to think about things like that. Things about death. But the black box flashed in her mind anyway.

Yolanda went to Wela's bedroom. Filtered beams of sunlight danced over Wela's still body, while the butterflies opened and closed their wings in her hair. She walked over to the bed and tucked a lock of white curls behind Wela's ear. Her eyes were closed.

"Wela?"

Silence.

She must have imagined it. There was no way Wela had spoken to her.

But then again, she had called her Violeta. . . . Yolanda wouldn't imagine something like that.

She turned her attention back to the old photograph on the vanity. The girl in the middle had to be Wela; she had the same wild curls as Yolanda. The older girl had to be Wela's sister, Violeta, and the boy hanging upside down was Wela's little brother, Raúl. Yolanda knew something terrible happened to them a long time ago, but Wela refused to talk about it. Why would Wela call her Violeta? And why would she say she was sorry? Sorry for what?

"Yolanda!" Mrs. Patel called.

Yolanda set the urn on the floor, pulled the black metal

box from the shelf, and carried it to the kitchen.

"I'm hoping Dad will be back by next weekend. I want to go on the camping trip," Sonja said.

Yolanda set the metal box on the table. "Why do you want to be in the boys camping club anyway?"

Sonja looked at her sister blankly. "It's not the *boys* camping club—it's just camping club."

"Whatever." Yolanda turned the lock toward Sonja. "Can you open this?"

Sonja reached into her pocket and pulled out a small pocketknife. She flipped open the knife, pulled out the toothpick, and jiggled at the lock. Within a few seconds, it clicked and popped open.

Yolanda shuffled through the papers, but there was nothing resembling a will in the box. "It doesn't look like she has a will." Yolanda's fingers brushed a book near the bottom.

"You girls need to head out. The bus will be here shortly." Mrs. Patel slung her bag over her shoulder. "Ghita and Hasik will meet you there. Once the nurse gets here for Josefa, I have to get back to the hospital."

Yolanda's heart prickled at Ghita's name. She hated to admit it, even to herself, but she really missed her best friend. Things had been so lonely without her for the last nine months. Even Yolanda's science fair project had suffered. It was nothing like the one she and Ghita had done together last year.

Sonja picked up her cereal-box-sized bee house and shoved it into her backpack.

Yolanda lifted the book and flipped through the pages, recognizing the slanted handwriting. It was Wela's journal. She tucked the book in her backpack, grabbed her poster board, opened the screen door to the backyard, and shouted, "Rosalind Franklin, get in here!"

Their home was set on a few thousand acres in the town of McClintock in southern New Mexico, in the valley of the Organ Mountains. From the porch, all the way to the old riverbed, it was flat, dry, and dusty, dotted with long arms of ocotillo and sagebrush. The April winds had finally calmed, and now that is was May, the air was clearer than it had been a few weeks ago. It was so clear, Yolanda could see all the way to where the last pecan tree stood. When Wela was a child, the land was covered in thousands and thousands of pecan trees. Then the drought came fifty years ago and killed most of them. There was only one pecan tree left, but it never blossomed anymore. It stood atop a tall, isolated hill with steep sides and a flat top that the towns-folk called Brujas Butte. Yolanda and her family just called it the butte because Wela forbade them to even mutter the word "*bruja*" in her presence. The word meant "witch," and if Wela ever heard they girls say it, it would get them a raised *chancla* and a long list of chores.

Rosalind Franklin scampered up the steps and into the house as Yolanda slammed the screen door behind her.

"You aren't going to call for Yosemite?" Sonja asked, her eyes blazing.

Yolanda shrugged and walked out the front door.

Three

THE BUS would be there any minute, and Yolanda needed to look busy before Hasik and Ghita arrived. She didn't want Ghita to think she was missing her.

Even though she was.

It had been hard to work on her science fair project alone this year. Last year she and Ghita had powered a small clock with the energy from an ordinary potato. They had won second place. When their names were announced, they screamed so loud and hugged so tight. Yolanda missed that. She missed Ghita. Without her, she had no one.

Yolanda sat alone on a boulder in front of their mailbox, clutching her poster board and the box of plastic cups containing her remaining fruit flies. She double-checked the lids on each one, making sure they were secure. The project had been disastrous from the start, and Yolanda had taken forever to decide what topic to choose. Ghita was usually the one who would push Yolanda in one direction. Without her, Yolanda was a little lost.

For her project this year she'd wanted to map out the crossings of different eye colors in fruit flies, but it hadn't gone well. Rosalind Franklin had knocked over her first set of cups, letting the fruit flies loose in the house. Wela had not been happy and made Yolanda move her project to the workshop. The second round had gone a bit better, but one night the temperature dropped too low and most of her flies had died. But there were a few left in her cups and she was able to get most of the data she needed. Still, she couldn't help but feel like things would have gone smoother had Ghita been her partner.

She pressed her earbuds into her ears and flicked to her favorite podcast: *The Science Minute*. Ten minutes of a new science topic every morning. Today they were discussing the relationship between genes and the environment.

"Our genes do not determine who we are by themselves. They work with the environment, our life experiences, the food we eat, the things that have happened to us to determine who we are. Humans are made up of a complicated dance between nature—

our genes—and nurture—the environment."

Yolanda pulled an eraser from her backpack, fixed a stray pencil mark on her poster, and held it up.

Perfect.

Although her friendship with Ghita had begun over science, Ghita hadn't been the one to introduce Yolanda to her love of the subject. That had been Welo. After he retired from being a professor at the college, he kept himself busy with new research projects. He let Yolanda hang around and put her to work helping prepare slides. He talked to her about all sorts of things: plants, animals, genetics. Welo had spent most of his life trying to solve the mystery behind the special family trait. He had been desperate to figure out how to explain it in some way so that people would understand why Wela was special. A few weeks before his death, Welo gripped Yolanda's hand, his eyes wild. "Yo," he had whispered. "It's in the *casita*. Take her back to the tree." He was so sick by then and Yolanda had no idea who or what he was talking about. She had never even been to the *casita* before; it was way out on their property. She was sure he didn't even know what he was saying anymore. His eyes darted to Wela sleeping beside him. "I hope your Wela forgave me for what I did. I should have taken her back myself. I never should have done it." Yolanda had gently shushed him back to sleep, terrified he might say something more. He closed his eyes and whispered, "Promise me you'll take her. Take her to the tree."

"I promise. I promise, Welo," she had said just to calm him.

She still didn't know what he'd been so frantic about, and she felt terrible for not being able to keep that promise.

Yolanda glanced up.

Sonja stood near the dirt road, bouncing up and down, her backpack poking out at an odd angle from the humming bee house wedged inside. A few stray bees buzzed around her braids. Yolanda laughed to herself. *Nice try, Sonja. The bus driver is still going to notice that.*

Ghita and Hasik jogged down the dirt road from their house, which was a two-minute walk up the road. The Patels were the only other family who lived on Rowley Road and the only family in town who would socialize with Wela and the girls. They owned a small bit of land with an enormous greenhouse out back where Mr. Patel grew all the plants he sold at his nursery in town. When Sonja spotted Ghita and Hasik, she smiled and stopped bouncing. She was always like that around Ghita.

Smiling.

It was hard to see Ghita and Sonja together. It used to be Yolanda and Ghita. And now it was Sonja and Ghita.

All the time.

Yolanda stole a glance at Hasik. He was at least two heads taller than Sonja, with a muscular, stocky build. He was probably the strongest kid in their class, and the kindest. Yolanda hadn't spoken to him since the day she found Wela on the floor of her workshop and ran to their house for help. Towering over Ghita and Sonja, he held his poster board and a gnarled root in one hand and waved awkwardly with his other. Yolanda smiled. He was a nice boy.

Ghita placed a box containing three yellow pots overloaded with fuchsia blooms on the ground. She was tiny and thin, completely opposite of her brother. She revealed a bouquet of wildflowers from behind her back; the buds were all tightly closed and new. Ghita plucked a yellow bud from the bunch and held it out for Sonja. Sonja touched her fingertip to the bud and its petals stretched wide.

That's new, Yolanda thought. She hadn't seen Sonja work with plants before. *Her skill must be getting stronger.* Even though the butterflies were always with Wela, she could do all sorts of things with other insects too. And plants. Wela rescued plants that were well past their prime from Mr. Patel's nursery and brought them back to life with the touch of her fingertip.

Sonja smelled the yellow flower before handing it back, and Ghita stood on tiptoes and wove it into Sonja's braids. They repeated this a few times, Sonja opening the closed bud and Ghita weaving it into her hair, making a colorful crown for the bees to fly around in. Sonja's cheeks flushed pink.

Ghita thinks she's so cool now because of that ring in her nose, thought Yolanda. She had gotten it during a trip to India last fall. Everyone, except Yolanda, had surrounded her at school, commenting that it was awesome her mother let her get her nose pierced.

Ghita brushed her long dark hair behind her shoulder and pulled out an orange flute with a large bulb on one end. She played a cheerful tune while Sonja danced and laughed and the bees flew in a circle around the both of them.

When the bus rumbled down the dusty road, Yolanda turned off her podcast, tossed her phone in her backpack, and picked up her poster and box of cups.

A stray bee flew by her face, and she let go of the poster to flick it away.

The air rushing from the approaching bus caught the poster and sucked it underneath. She dropped the box of cups on the ground, and one of the cups rolled underneath the bus, cracking under the tire.

No! No! No!

A wave of panic coursed through her body. She reached for the poster, but it disappeared and then popped out from the massive black tires as the brakes squealed to a halt in a cloud of dust.

"No!" Yolanda dashed after it, but the wind picked up, rolling the poster down the dirt road. Her heart sank. This couldn't be happening. Not today. Not after all her hard work.

Hasik thundered past her and snatched the poster off the ground. "Here you go—" He handed her the crumpled poster, a look of pity on his face.

"Thanks," she muttered. The poster was ripped down the center and covered with black tire marks. She picked up her one remaining cup. Three red-eyed fruit flies buzzed around inside. This couldn't be happening. Not today, not right now.

Sonja glanced back and bounded up the steps after Ghita, seemingly unaware that this was all her fault.

"Oh no you don't," the bus driver called.

"What?" Sonja said.

"No bees on the bus! I don't know how many times we have to go through this—I can see the box in your backpack."

The color drained from Sonja's face.

The bus driver pointed and shook his head again. "*Bruja*," he muttered.

Sonja's shoulders slumped in disappointment.

"I'll walk with you," Ghita said as they stepped off the bus and started toward school.

Hasik walked up the steps and Yolanda followed. *I knew he was going to catch you,* Yolanda thought. A few bees, left behind, flew into her face. This time, unable to resist, she flicked hard at one and it came back and stung her on the cheek.

"Ouch!" She slapped her palm to her face. Her heart began to pound as she realized what she had done.

No! Not again!

She froze. Her heart thumped in her chest.

"Take your seat," the bus driver grumbled under his stiff white mustache as he swatted a bee from his face.

Hasik turned around. "Are you coming?"

Yolanda stumbled back from the bus, already feeling dizzy. Hasik came down the steps and walked toward her.

"Are you coming or not?" the bus driver yelled. When neither of them answered, he shut the door and the bus shuddered down the road.

Her cheek was already beginning to swell.

She dumped the contents from her backpack on the ground. *Where is it? Where is it?* She found the box and ripped it open, her heart jumping in her throat. She had to hurry. She didn't have much time.

"What's wrong?" Hasik said.

Calm. She had to stay calm. A rapid heartbeat would spread the venom faster. Her eye was starting to swell shut. White spots entered her vision.

She tried to screw the injector together, but her hands were shaking too badly.

She needed to get the stinger out.

Her eyelids fluttered. She fell back from the dizziness, her throat beginning to squeeze closed.

"Oh no." Hasik towered over her, his face panic-stricken. "I don't know what to do. Tell me what to do."

"Bees—aller—" She handed him the injector.

His brown eyes were the last thing she saw, just before everything went dark.

Four

YOLANDA gasped for air and her eyes shot open. A single brown eye loomed over her face. Her heart thumped in her chest.

"Got it!" Hasik held a tiny stinger in between his fingers. "That's what I'm supposed to do, right? Get the stinger out?"

"Yep," Sonja said as she pulled the injector out of Yolanda's thigh.

Yolanda rubbed her itchy swollen cheek, sat up, and looked around. She was sitting in the middle of Rowley Road. She couldn't believe it had happened—again.

"Should we call Mrs. Patel?" Sonja stuffed the injector into Yolanda's backpack and stood.

"I'm trying to get her." Ghita pressed her phone to her ear.

Yolanda's head swam. "I should have allergy pills in my bag. Can you get me one?"

Hasik dug around in her backpack until he found the bottle of pills and handed her one. Then he showed her the bulbous orange root. "This can help with swelling. It's turmeric." He scratched it against the ground, brushed off the dirt, and handed it to her. The exposed root glistened a deep burnt orange.

"Thanks." Yolanda rubbed it over the raw part of her cheek. The cool juice was soothing. She tried to relax and close her eyes, but she still felt itchy all over.

"I can't get my mom!" Ghita pressed her phone to her ear, frantically pacing back and forth in the middle of the road. "She's not answering!"

Ghita never was calm in emergency situations. Yolanda almost wanted to laugh, but then a wave of dizziness swept over her and she lay back again.

"You woke up right away." Sonja blocked the morning sun, casting a shadow over Yolanda. "Just like last time." She slung her backpack over her shoulder. Bees buzzed all around her. "I can try to find someone to help if you want."

"No, no." Yolanda climbed to her feet. "You've done enough. Just stay away from me." Yolanda's head swam again. She stumbled backward, and Hasik helped her regain her balance. Sonja gazed down at her feet and cinched her backpack up on her shoulders. It was clear she felt terrible about the bees. Yolanda picked up her ripped poster and plastic cup from the ground. She checked that her three remaining fruit flies were still alive and stowed the cup in her backpack. She folded the poster and tucked it underneath her arm. "I've got to get to the science fair."

"Are you sure?" Hasik raised an eyebrow. "I think you can get excused. This seems pretty serious."

"I'm fine." Yolanda brushed her curls out of her face. "I need to get away from the bees. That's all."

Sonja and Ghita exchanged a look. Yolanda's stomach pinched as she looked away. Why did they always do that, exchange looks like she couldn't see?

Sonja and Ghita hung back while Hasik and Yolanda started down the dusty dirt road toward school. It was a three-mile walk. There were no trees in sight, only dry desert grasses and the occasional patch of cactus with waving green paddles covered in yellow spines to mark their progress.

"How many times have you been stung?" Hasik asked.

"Too many to count."

"That was pretty scary. You were gone"—he snapped his fingers—"just like that."

"I know."

She didn't like to be out of control of her body. The way the dizziness took over, the way she knew she was going to pass out . . . It was terrifying.

"It must be hard living with Sonja and the bees."

"Yeah. I try to avoid them, but sometimes . . ." She didn't know what else to say. There wasn't anything she could do about it, so why bother talking about it?

When they got to the bottom of the road, they passed Mr. Patel's nursery. The rusted sign hung crooked on the front door, the white paint chipped from the harsh desert winds.

"I'm sorry about your grandmother," Hasik said, a hint of sadness in his voice.

Not this. Anything but this.

Yolanda had run straight to the Patel house when she found Wela on the floor of her workshop. Hasik had been so calm, calling 911 and staying by her side until the ambulance came.

"Thanks," mumbled Yolanda.

"You know, I lost my Nani—my grandmother—late last summer. It was awful. Mom took me and Ghita to visit her in India and she just . . . died. She was sick, but it was still unexpected. She was a famous snake charmer, and all these people came to her funeral to pay their respects. I was—"

"Wela's not dead, Hasik." This talk about death was making her uncomfortable. "Besides, I don't want to talk about it." Thinking about the possibility of Wela dying made her dizzy again.

"Okay. I'm sorry though."

She nodded and felt bad for snapping at him. She knew he wasn't trying to pry, but she didn't like to talk about those sad, awful things all the time. Lately, she was surrounded by sadness.

"If you ever want to talk about it. Or your grandfather—he died late last summer too, didn't he?"

Yolanda's heart sank. She definitely didn't want to talk about that.

Ever.

She swallowed the lump in her throat and blinked back tears. She didn't say anything, as it might have caused her carefully hidden emotions to spill over. She would be horrified if Hasik ever saw her cry.

"I'm sorry," Hasik said again, shaking his head. "I didn't mean to . . ." He shrugged, and they continued trudging down the road in silence, the only sounds their shoes scraping against the dirt road and the hot breeze in their ears.

The auditorium roared with the chatter and laughter of students and teachers milling around and enjoying the science fair posters. Yolanda spotted a small crowd around Sonja and Ghita's poster. The three yellow pots overflowing with pink blooms were set up in front, a small crowd gathered around them as Ghita pulled out the flute and began to play a song.

Yolanda strode behind the crowd and watched as Sonja dipped tiny spoons into different jars of honey, letting people taste each variety. Eli Jensen and another boy stood in front of her.

"I heard they are 'together,'" Eli said, making quotes with his fingers.

"Like girlfriends?" the other boy said. Eli shrugged and then laughed.

Yolanda's stomach lurched. She didn't like overhearing things she wasn't supposed to, especially about Sonja and Ghita. She was about to walk away.

"If it wasn't for those bees . . ." Eli rubbed his jaw. The other boy laughed.

Yolanda couldn't help herself. "What?" she snapped. "What? If it wasn't for the bees . . ."

Eli turned around, the color drained from his face. "Sorry, Yo. I didn't realize you were right there."

"No, no." Yolanda crossed her arms over her chest. "If

it wasn't for the bees . . . what? Sonja would be your girl-friend?"

"Uhhhh," Eli said, a dumb look on his face. The other boy laughed.

"Fat chance. I don't think so. She's way too smart to like someone like you. Besides, isn't it *your* mother trying to keep her out of camping club? Why? Can't handle a girl who can put up a tent?"

"Oh!" The other boy threw his head back and laughed.

"Now, wait a second, Yo." Eli pointed a finger at her. "That's not fair. You know it's because of the bees."

She shook her head, knowing it was more than the bees. It was the way Eli's mother and grandmother looked at Wela and Sonja every time they were in the grocery store, bending their heads together and whispering that word: *bruja.* "I live with the bees, Eli. Get over yourself."

The other boy covered his mouth and laughed.

"What happened to your face?" Eli glared at her. "Did a *bruja* get you?"

Yolanda's stomach tightened at that word. She almost expected Wela to come around the corner with her *chancla* raised. She clenched her jaw, dug deep, and walked away.

Why was everyone in this town so awful to their family? And why didn't Wela and Welo just leave if they obviously weren't welcome here?

She strode in front of her sister's poster while Ghita waved her arms wildly about, explaining the effects the music had on the amounts of honey the two different colonies were able to produce. Mr. Green, the science teacher and judge of the science fair, smiled as he licked the tiny spoon clean.

She sulked over to where she was supposed to set up her poster and tossed her backpack on the table. Her project was ruined, but she had to do something. She couldn't leave it the way it was. Mr. Green was her favorite teacher after all. He had this way of explaining the world that just made so much sense to her.

Engrossed in her work, she didn't notice when Hasik came up behind her, until he tapped her on the shoulder. She looked up, her eye and cheek so swollen she could hardly see him.

"Whoa! That one got you good." He smiled his bright white smile and then scrunched up his face. Hasik jumped on the table next to her, swinging his legs. He pulled out a black pen and started helping her fill in the words.

"What's this?" Yolanda pointed to his handwriting.

"Is something wrong? I'm not the best speller."

"I'll say."

"Hey," Hasik protested.

Yolanda pointed at the poster. "There's no 'f' in 'drosophila,' it's 'ph.' And mutant doesn't have an 'e' in it."

He shrugged and snapped his pen cap on with this thumb. "I tried."

Yolanda fixed the poster as best as she could, blowing the curls out of her face.

"You have cool hair," Hasik said. Then he rubbed the back of his head and his eyes darted toward the floor.

Yolanda couldn't help but feel the heat rise up the back of her neck. Her palms tingled as she tried to ignore it. Hasik smiled again, cleared his throat, and swung his legs. Yolanda shook her head, trying to erase the feeling, but it remained. Why was he making her feel like this?

She settled on leaving her poster flat on the table with the one remaining cup of fruit flies in front of it when Mr. Green approached the table and adjusted his glasses, his black wiry hair radiating in a million directions around his head.

"Yolanda. What happened here?" He tapped his clipboard with his pen. "I expected much greater work than this."

She froze, unable to speak.

Mr. Green leaned in and squinted at her. "What happened to your eye?"

"I got stung—" she started to say.

"Oh, the honeybees! Weren't they great? I love the

honey Sonja brought. She has a real winner with that project. Must run in the family."

Yolanda winced. Of course he liked Sonja's project more. That was how it always was, Sonja beating her at life.

"I expected more, Yolanda. I'm sorry to say this, but I'm disappointed."

"I—I—" Yolanda didn't know what to say. She wanted to tell him what happened, but the words weren't coming. She couldn't even think.

"She got stung by a bee and almost died," Hasik said, the usual smile missing from his face.

Mr. Green looked from Hasik to Yolanda. She nodded and found her voice. "My poster got smashed under the bus today. I got stung and I'm allergic."

"I'm sorry to hear that, Yolanda." Mr. Green adjusted his glasses. "Even though this is not what I would have liked to have seen from you." He leaned in. "Wow! Your eye is really swollen. Are you sure you're okay?"

She nodded and shrugged, covering her eye with her hand. *It must look really bad*, she thought.

Mr. Green glanced at the crumpled poster board. He picked up the plastic cup and looked at the contents before setting it down. "I'm sorry it's too late for the judging, but you may redo the poster and turn it in next week for a partial grade."

Yolanda swallowed hard and sat down, disappointment filling her. She shut her eyes. It wasn't what she was hoping for. She wouldn't win the science fair, but at least she wouldn't fail her favorite class. Mr. Green moved to the next student while Hasik jumped from the table.

"Come on. I want to show you my project." Hasik grabbed her hand and pulled her toward the other side of the auditorium. "It's on the healing properties of plants. I've got an aloe plant, turmeric, echinacea. Plants are so cool."

Yolanda walked behind him, dragging her feet before stealing another glance at the crowd around Sonja's poster.

Five

HASIK was turning over the turmeric root in his hands, smiling, as he told Yolanda about its anti-inflammatory properties, when Mr. Green made the announcement overhead.

"Attention, everyone. It's time to announce the winner of Elion Junior High's annual seventh-grade science fair."

Yolanda glanced at Sonja and Ghita, who stood next to each other, holding hands. Yolanda couldn't help but wish that she and Ghita were the ones standing next to each other.

Sonja was bouncing up and down again. The bee house was wedged inside Sonja's backpack under the table. A stray bee flew around her head, darting in and out of the crown of flowers in her hair.

Mr. Green waited for the auditorium to quiet down. "Our first-place winners are . . . Sanghita Patel and Sonja Rodríguez-O'Connell, with their project on the effects of music on honey production in bees." Mr. Green clapped his hands.

A sinking feeling washed over Yolanda. *No. No. No.* This couldn't be happening. This wasn't fair. Her palms started to sweat and her heart pounded.

Sonja walked to the front with her perfect red braids, her perfect bees, and her perfect poster. Her freckled cheeks shone as she and Ghita collected the award.

Yolanda wanted to cry. She had to get out of there now, or she might. Sulking back to her poster, she folded it in half and left the auditorium as fast as she could. It wasn't just that Sonja had ruined Yolanda's project, but now she had actually won the science fair.

Science was Yolanda's thing. And now Sonja had shown her up on that, too. Like she did with the family trait. Like she did with everything. It wasn't fair. Yolanda bit down hard on the inside of her swollen cheek when Sonja came out of the auditorium, juggling the plants, the bee house, and the poster. Yolanda picked up her own poster and shoved it into the garbage can. It didn't fit, but it didn't matter.

Sonja walked over to her. "Can you believe it, Yo? We

won." Sonja's eyes sparkled. "I wasn't expecting that."

"Mmm-hmm," Yolanda said, her arms crossed tightly over her chest. She kept her teeth clenched so she wouldn't say anything else. Or cry. She might cry.

"Wow, your eye is really swollen. I'm sorry about that." Sonja shifted the pots and the bee house. "Ghita had to get something from her locker. Do you mind?"

She shoved the three yellow pots toward Yolanda. Yolanda stepped back and let the plants fall to the ground. The ceramic pots shattered on the concrete, spilling dirt and fuchsia blooms everywhere.

"Yo!" Sonja shouted.

Yolanda held her hands up and walked backward. "I'm sure you can fix it, no problem. Just use your bees."

"We have to present these plants in two weeks at the finals!" Sonja cried, frantically scooping soil back into the pot fragments.

Yolanda turned and ran toward the road.

Yolanda trudged up the dirt road, replaying the science fair over and over again. How could Sonja and Ghita have won? Because of the bees? It wasn't fair Sonja had her own swarm of personal pollinators. How was she supposed to compete with that? Sonja showed her up time and time again. It wasn't fair.

As Yolanda stewed, the night before Wela fell into the sleep crept into her mind. She couldn't help but wonder if it was all her fault. They had argued. Yolanda had gotten so angry.

Yolanda and Rosalind Franklin had walked over to Wela's workshop, Rosalind Franklin grunting and snorting at every small plant along the way.

"Come on!" Yolanda held the workshop door open. "I don't have all night." The dog skittered in through the open door.

The thick hot air hit her square in the face. Yolanda stepped between the dimly lit shelves filled with rows of scientific journals, glass jars containing a variety of specimens, shadow boxes of pinned insects and butterflies, microscopes, and slides. An old black-and-white photograph of a young Wela, with her long curly hair adorned with butterflies, and Welo, with his flop of black hair, hung crooked on the wall. She stopped and straightened it, then rounded the corner in the main area of the workshop.

Wela sat on a stool, curled over an open notebook. Her electric-white hair cascaded down her back in ribbony curls to her hips, while the butterflies flew around her.

"Wela? I was loo—"

Wela looked up and then glanced at the corner of the room.

Sonja.

She held an orb of fat bumblebees between her palms, her tongue peeking from the corner of her mouth.

Yolanda shuddered. Bees. Why did it have to be bees?

Yolanda started toward Wela. "I'm looking for Welo's old notes. I thought they'd be where they usually are, but I can't find them."

Wela pressed her lips together and held her hand up. "I'm not giving you those. That research was a waste of his time. And mine."

Yolanda groaned. "He was trying to help. He just wanted to make your life better." Yolanda gestured toward Sonja, who was concentrating hard on her bees. "He wanted to make our lives better."

Wela's eyes narrowed. "Your Welo did some truly awful things because of that thought."

"What thought?" Yolanda asked. She found it hard to believe that Welo had done anything awful.

"The thought that if he could figure out how to explain this family and the way we are, that somehow it would fix things. I'll tell you what: It doesn't matter why we are the way we are. *They* don't care." Wela pointed toward town. She was talking about the townsfolk, the rumors, the whispers.

"Then why do you stay? Why do we live here?" Yolanda said. "If it's so bad, then why don't we leave?" Rosalind

Franklin licked the sweat dripping down the back of her leg, and Yolanda shook her off. "Stop it, Rosalind Franklin!"

The dog lowered her ears, and Yolanda immediately felt bad for scolding her. She bent down to pet her when she spotted the trash can. The corner of a familiar green notebook was poking out. She walked over to it and pulled out the charred remains of a notebook.

"What did you do?" Yolanda reached inside and pulled out another piece of singed cardboard. Her heart began to race. She pulled out piece after piece, charred and ruined. It couldn't be. "These were his notes!"

"It's time we forget about his research." Wela closed her eyes.

"But this was his life's work!"

"It's over. Now, just forget about it."

Sonja grunted from the corner as the orb of bees began to break apart. "Yo! You broke my concentration!"

The bees zoomed around the room. One flew by Yolanda's ear. She ducked.

"You shouldn't be in here." A look of alarm came over Wela's face. "It's too dangerous."

"I can't believe you would do that!" The tears welled in Yolanda's eyes. Welo had been working for years trying to figure out what he could about the family trait. He always helped Wela with her work, the butterflies, all the years of research. How could she burn it all? Why would she do that?

Wela pointed at the door as another bee buzzed right past Yolanda's head. She ducked again.

"Why do you spend so much time with her? Why not me?" Yolanda's heart began to beat faster, and the familiar tightness in her chest squeezed so hard she couldn't breathe. "Because I didn't get one? Is that why?" The rage surged down her arms and out her fingertips. Her heart thumped in her chest, and it took everything in her not to scream.

"If only we had helped him!" She flicked an old pile of spiral notebooks from the counter, letting the loose papers flutter to the ground. "Maybe he could have finished his work and they wouldn't hate us."

Wela shook her head and held out her arms, her voice softened. "There are some things you will understand in time, *mija*. But right now . . . right now you have to trust me."

"Trust you? How could I? Look what you've done!" Yolanda kicked over the trash can full of the charred remains and walked out into the cool desert night, leaving Wela and Sonja alone in the workshop.

With the bees.

Six

THE HEAT radiated up from the asphalt, a wiggling
mirage in the distance. The sky was vast and blue, the
kind of blue that reminded Yolanda of the turquoise
stone at her neck. Her fingertips brushed across the
smooth stone of the bolo tie. She and Sonja had bought
it for Welo for his birthday to match the turquoise on
his rattlesnake-skin belt. Yolanda had worn it every day
since he died. Her heart ached when she thought of him
being gone forever and of Wela lying in the very same
bed, dying. She would never get to ask him another
question or help him feed the butterflies. She would
never get to help him in the workshop again. And now

it was looking like she wasn't going to get to do that with Wela either.

Her breath quickened as she walked along the pavement toward Rowley Road. Before making the turn up the dusty road, she passed by Mr. Patel's nursery. The sun was hot, and beads of sweat moistened the back of her neck. A ruby-colored car drove by, kicking up a cloud of dust as its wheels crunched along the road. Someone coughed. She turned around.

Hasik. His sneakers were untied and his brow was glistening in the heat.

Yolanda stopped. "Are you following me?"

He looked up. "You dropped this." He held out his hand. It was her poster. "And I also live on this road."

"I didn't drop it." She crossed her arms, turned around, and continued walking.

He jogged to catch up to her, his shoes scraping against the dirt. "You worked hard on it, and you're going to need it for the redo." Hasik held out his hand until she took the poster from him.

She stuffed it into her backpack.

"Your shoes are untied," Yolanda said.

Hasik stopped to tie them. Then he ran to catch up with her. "So, what's your thing? Your gift?"

"I have no idea what you are talking about." She wasn't

supposed to talk about that. Ever. Wela had made that abundantly clear. She continued trudging up the dirt road.

The trait was supposed to be a secret. A family secret Wela made sure she and Sonja knew not to talk about in front of anyone. But the townsfolk were not so easy to avoid.

Whenever someone heard that Yolanda and Sonja were Josefa Rodríguez's granddaughters, they grew too curious, and inevitably the conversation turned to Wela's butterflies and whether or not the rumors of the *brujas* were true. Then they would ask why Wela brought the drought.

Yolanda had grown so angry one time, she yelled at the school secretary that it was none of her business. The secretary told the principal, who called Wela. Wela had arrived in a fury, the butterflies following her right into the building. After she'd had a word with the principal and explained that she only studied butterflies, she'd told Yolanda that she needed to be more careful.

"We cannot lose our temper with these people. And we cannot tell them the truth. The butterflies are my science experiments only," Wela had said. "The truth is too dangerous."

She had made Yolanda promise not to talk about it with other people again.

"Oh, come on," Hasik said. "My dad has been supplying

your grandmother with milkweed for years. The butterflies are always around her, in her hair—I know they aren't just for research or whatever she says. And the plants? How does she bring them back to life like that? I told my dad he should hire her to work at the nursery." Hasik chuckled. "And Sonja? The bees? It's kind of hard to ignore."

Yolanda dug her fingernails into her palms. Wela would freak out if she heard Hasik talking about this. But then again, Wela was asleep—and maybe dying. Yolanda shuddered.

"I tried to get Ghita to tell me, but she won't say a word."

At least she kept one promise, Yolanda thought, pursing her lips. *What's the point of all the secrets anyway? Who cares if he knows?*

"I didn't get a gift," Yolanda said simply.

"Oh."

"Yeah."

"That's a bummer."

"I don't know . . . I guess it should bother me—but it doesn't." Yolanda could feel the lie bubbling up in her gut, threatening to expose her. Of course she wanted one. Why wouldn't she want one? It's what was supposed to make her a Rodríguez.

"Oh man, that would bother me." Hasik shook his head.

"If Ghita had a cool gift and I didn't, I'd be mad."

"Well, that's the difference between you and me, then." Yolanda tightened the straps on her backpack and picked up her pace.

Hasik held his arms out. "Aren't you going to walk with me?"

"Why?" Yolanda called over her shoulder.

"Because I returned your poster."

"So?"

"So I returned your poster, and most people would be thankful and maybe talk to the other person."

"Fine—" Yolanda paused, waiting for him to catch up. "Gosh, you can be really annoying."

Hasik smiled. His bright white teeth glowed against his brown skin, and Yolanda felt a pinch in her stomach. He didn't seem bothered by her calling him annoying. "What happened between you and Ghita? Why aren't you friends anymore?" he asked.

Yolanda looked at him blankly. He was so nosy.

"Let me guess—you don't want to talk about it?" Hasik cocked his head from side to side playfully.

Yolanda crossed her arms over her chest. "No, I don't."

"Okay, okay but"—his voice softened—"she really misses you."

She does? Yolanda thought hopefully. Then she shook

her head. "She has Sonja now. She doesn't miss me. And I don't miss her."

"I thought you didn't want to talk about it."

"I don't! *You* are talking about it."

"Fine. No problem." Hasik held up his hands in defeat. "We can talk about something else." Hasik lowered his voice. "Let's talk about something non-controversial. Like—what are you doing this afternoon?"

Yolanda breathed a sigh of relief and started to walk again. She wanted to lie, but for some reason, even though he was pushy and slightly annoying, Hasik was kind and she felt comfortable with him. "I want to see if there is any update on my dad. He was supposed to be coming home, but they called him for a dangerous mission in Afghanistan a few weeks ago. We haven't heard anything."

She'd been waiting for a call. He always called. But so far there had been no word.

Mamá and Dad had met in the army, on their first tour of Afghanistan. After Mamá died giving birth to the girls, Dad had gone back every few years on mission after mission, leaving the girls in the care of their *abuelos*.

The morning he left the last time, Yolanda pulled the blue star flag from the drawer and handed it to him.

"You hang it," she said, stone-faced. "Since you are leaving us again."

Her dad took the flag from her, touched the shiny blue star in the center, and kneeled in front of her. "Yolanda, this is my last tour. I promise." His face looked different. The reddish beard that had covered his face over the past few months was gone. He didn't even look like her dad anymore.

The lump in her throat kept her from being able to speak. If she spoke, she might cry. She crossed her arms and waited.

Her dad stood up.

"You can't leave now. Not after—Welo." Yolanda clamped her mouth shut. She really didn't want to cry. "If you leave—then you hang it." She had never asked him to stay before, but she'd been certain there was no way he would leave them. How could he? After everything they had just gone through?

Her dad sighed and wiped the sweat from his naked pale cheek. He walked to the window and hung the flag. Then he picked up his desert camouflage bag, slung it over his shoulder, and kissed Yolanda on the cheek. "I have a duty."

Yolanda stood stiff and stunned. How could he do this? How could he leave them at a time like this?

"I'll take it down when I get back, and we can put it away for the last time," he said. "Promise." He touched her shoulder lightly and squeezed it just so before walking through the kitchen and out of her life.

Yolanda watched from the window, tears finally streaming down her cheeks. Rosalind Franklin anxiously licked at them. Wela and Sonja sent him off with tears, hugs, and kisses at the front door. Her dad briefly looked up at the window, a solemn expression on his face, before climbing into his truck and driving away.

"My mom didn't say anything about your dad," Hasik said. "I'm sorry."

She blinked tears back and cleared her throat. She couldn't think about him now. Who knew where he was or what was happening to him this time. "And I have to avoid Sonja. And her bees." She touched the raw spot on her cheek.

He rubbed the back of his head with his hand. "That stinks," he said. "And your eye looks really—"

Yolanda glanced up at him. "Terrible?"

"Well—yeah." Hasik smiled, and the tightness in her chest relaxed a little. "I have an aloe plant I can bring over. It can help with the swelling. I've actually read honey can help with bee stings as well."

"Honey?" she scoffed. "Yeah, right."

Seven

WHEN they reached Yolanda's house, she felt a little better. Hasik was easy to talk to, even if he was a little pushy. A ruby sedan was parked in the driveway next to a white car.

"I wonder who that is." Yolanda craned her neck to see inside the red car. No one was there. "The nurse drives the white car."

"Maybe they sent someone else today," Hasik said. They walked along a gravel path between the side of the house and the small detached garage that was Wela's workshop. "My mom said she's going to bring dinner over tonight."

Mrs. Patel was always doing things like that after Welo

died, bringing food over and checking on Wela. Especially after Dad left.

As they rounded the corner to the backyard, Yolanda stopped in her tracks.

"What the—?"

A fine layer of green covered the desert backyard, as far as she could see—all the way to the riverbed.

"Whoa, look at that." Hasik walked to the edge, bent down, and skimmed his hands over the top. It was only a few inches tall.

Yolanda bent down to do the same. "That's so strange." The young blades were soft between her fingers.

Hasik walked out into it. "It's beautiful," he said. "But . . . it hasn't rained in ages." Hasik bent down and examined it again. Closer this time. "You've never had grass back here before, have you?"

Yolanda shook her head. The backyard had always been the same, a barren desert of ocotillo, cactus, and sage, but nothing exceptionally green. Not this green. Sonja said there were cottonwoods by the riverbed, but most of those were long dead from the drought.

"Hmmm." Hasik was on all fours now, peering at the grass. "Did they used to grow anything here? It sure is a lot of land to not use it for anything."

"Wela's family used to have a pecan orchard here. But

that was a long time ago." Yolanda pointed in the hazy distance toward the butte. "That tree is the last one, although it never blooms. Wela's whole family is buried there." Even Mamá.

Yolanda had tried to ask Wela about it once, but Wela snapped at her. "Don't talk to me about that tree!" Yolanda and Sonja had exchanged a look, and neither of them had mentioned it again.

Rosalind Franklin barked from inside the house, and Yolanda climbed the steps to let her out. She scampered through the screen door, leapt off the wraparound porch, and bolted into the grass. The tags on her collar clinked as she pranced through the grass.

"Rosalind Franklin!" Yolanda called. The dog's ears perked up, but she ignored Yolanda and continued sniffing the grass.

"Your dog has a first and last name?" Hasik cocked his head to the side. "I like it."

Yolanda smiled and brushed her curls from her face. "Rosalind Franklin is my favorite scientist. Wela told me about her right around the time we got our dogs and I couldn't get her out of my mind, so . . ."

Hasik smiled. "Makes perfect sense."

Rosalind Franklin limped over, lifted her front paw, and whined. Yolanda picked her up and found a fat goathead burr lodged deep in the pad. When she gripped it between her fingers and tugged, Rosalind Franklin yelped and jerked her paw away.

"Hang on, girl. Lemme get it."

She tried again, and this time it pulled loose but stuck in her own thumb. She winced. She carefully pulled it out and set Rosalind Franklin on the ground.

"You're lucky I like you." Yolanda sucked the blood from her thumb. The little black dog wagged her tail thankfully and danced around her in a circle.

From Wela's workshop, there was a crash.

"What was that?" Yolanda said.

Rosalind Franklin bolted for the cracked door, and Hasik and Yolanda followed her inside, stepping between the darkened shelves. Rosalind Franklin's barks echoed in the workshop. On one of the shelves Yolanda spotted Welo's machete next to a stuffed bobcat with pointed black ears, its sharp teeth bared. She had always hated that thing. Welo used to tease the girls and hide it in unexpected places. Wela found it once and it scared her so bad she threw it out, but Welo dug it out from the garbage and put it back on the shelf. Now no one had the heart to throw it out.

Yolanda picked up the machete.

When they entered the main part of the workshop, a woman with her hair in a tight blond bun stood on a stool in the center of the room, holding a notebook. Rosalind Franklin jumped and barked, nipping at her shoes.

"Oh! Thank goodness! Can you get this dog away from me?" The woman shook a manicured hand at Rosalind Franklin, who jumped up and tried to bite it. "I'm terribly frightened of dogs."

"Who are you?" Yolanda held the machete up. "And what are you doing in here?"

The woman straightened her blouse, almost losing her balance on the stool. She regained her balance and stuck out her hand. "I'm Abby Malcolm. Social worker."

"Oh." Yolanda didn't move. She'd forgotten that Mrs. Patel said a social worker was coming by.

"You must be Yolanda?" Abby checked her notebook. "Or are you Sonja?"

"Yolanda."

"Great! It's a pleasure to meet you. Do you think you can get your dog to stop trying to attack me?" Rosalind Franklin jumped and scratched at the stool, and Abby clutched the notebook to her chest, a terrified look on her face.

"Rosalind Franklin! Get over here," Yolanda said. When Rosalind Franklin didn't stop, Yolanda set the machete on a shelf and picked up her fat, wiggling body. She handed the dog to Hasik.

Abby stepped down from the stool and tugged her skirt down. "That's better," she said. "I knocked on the front door, but the nurse said you weren't here. She said sometimes you all are in the workshop, so . . . Anyhow, that's how I ended up in here." She consulted her notebook again. "I've been trying to get ahold of your father, but it's been tricky getting in touch with him."

"He's on an important mission."

"Appears to be the case. So, we need to figure out where to send you and your sister until he gets back. Shreya Patel, your neighbor, said she's been the main caregiver for you all since your grandmother became ill. Do you have any other family nearby?"

"You aren't sending us anywhere." Yolanda crossed her arms over her chest.

"Oh, honey, I know this is hard. I do. I really do." She placed a hand on Yolanda's shoulder. Yolanda shook her off and took a step back. *You don't know anything about us.*

Abby stooped down to her eye level, and Yolanda clenched her arms across her chest even tighter. Abby removed her glasses. "I understand this is hard and scary, but you have to understand, you and your sister are twelve years old. You are kids. You can't live in this house with your grandmother the way she is . . . all alone. It's not a safe situation."

Yolanda knew Abby was right, but she wasn't going to give her an inch. Some stranger wasn't going to get to choose what happened to everyone in her family.

"We don't have other family. Wela is our only family . . . who sticks around." Yolanda felt a little pang of guilt when she said that and thought of her dad.

"What about any family friends?"

Yolanda glanced at Hasik, who hadn't said anything. He shifted uncomfortably. "I'm sure my mom would love to help, but we leave for India in a couple days. My aunt is getting married."

"Why can't we do what we've been doing? Mrs. Patel checks on us throughout the day and makes us food sometimes. Why can't we do that until my dad gets home?"

"Because . . . that's not a long-term solution, and Mrs. Patel is leaving the country. If your dad were coming home tomorrow, that would be one thing. But the military told me it could be weeks before we hear from his unit. So, we need to plan accordingly. I'll be back tomorrow afternoon, when the hospice home comes to pick up your grandmother—"

"Wela!" Yolanda snapped. If they couldn't even get her name right, how would they ensure she would be taken care of? How could Wela be going to hospice? Didn't they understand she was just asleep? She had to be asleep, or else all of this was Yolanda's fault.

Abby reviewed her notes. "She's being transferred to Meitner Place. They will take good care of your grandmother—I mean Wela. I'll be here at two o'clock tomorrow, when they come to pick her up, and you and Sonja both need to have your bags packed. We will have to place you somewhere."

"But what about our dogs?" Yolanda hadn't considered what would happen to Rosalind Franklin or Yosemite. "And where? Who will we have to go with?"

"You can have a friend care for the dogs." Abby glanced at Rosalind Franklin and wrinkled her nose. "Or surrender them to the shelter."

"Surrender them? Abandon her?" Yolanda took Rosalind Franklin from Hasik and rubbed the soft spot between her eyes. Rosalind Franklin immediately relaxed. Yolanda's chest squeezed tight. "I'm never doing that."

"I'm so sorry. I really am." Abby tried to touch Yolanda's arm, but Rosalind Franklin nipped at her hand and Abby jumped back. She closed her eyes and took a deep breath. "This is not a safe situation for you and your sister. You cannot live here with your grandmother the way she is. It's too big of a job for you girls."

"We've been doing just fine."

"Yes, yes, you are right. You have been doing a great job. But we need to make some hard decisions. And it's easier if we do that together, with all of the cards on the table." Abby checked her watch and pressed her notebook to her chest. "I have one more question. I apologize if you think this rude, but what is this I've heard about"—Abby lowered her voice—"a *bruja*?"

There was that word again. The anger bubbled up inside of Yolanda as she stared at Abby blankly and said nothing. Abby didn't know what she was talking about, it was obvious, but Yolanda wasn't going to dignify her question with a response.

"I'm sorry. Some folks at the office were talking about it. I wasn't sure what it meant and I just moved here. . . ." Abby glanced down at her watch. "I'm sorry, I have another appointment. Tomorrow. Two o'clock."

Yolanda squeezed Rosalind Franklin to her chest and nuzzled her nose in the dog's fur. She was not going to get rid of her dog, and she and Sonja were not going to foster care. There was no way she was going to let any of that happen.

Eight

LATER that evening, as the sun was setting, Yolanda let Rosalind Franklin into the backyard and watched as she bolted to the edge of the grass, sniffing along the edge. The grass had grown in the few hours since she and Hasik first noticed it. She bent down and skimmed her fingertips over the top. It was to her knees.

Pop. Click. Pop.

How strange. It was the sound of the grass growing.

She had been told very little about their family history, the town of McClintock, and Wela's relationship with the townsfolk. But over the years, bits leaked out here and there. Like the time Eli's mother called Wela about Sonja's bees and the camping trip. When they hung up, Wela muttered under her breath, "*Por el árbol se conoce el fruto.*" Yolanda didn't know exactly what it meant, but she knew it was something about children being like their parents. Up until Welo died, Wela had always been vague about growing up here. She had told them before the drought it used to be a pecan orchard and that her family owned it and worked on it. The girls knew she'd had a brother and a sister and assumed she had a mother and father too, but the details were always incomplete.

And of course she had heard the rumors all over town about how Wela had caused the drought fifty years ago when she and Welo moved back to the orchard. The strange looks. The mothers who held back their children and whispered when Wela passed by, the butterflies winking in her hair. They whispered that word under their breath.

Bruja.

Wela spent most of her time holed up in her lab at the college or in her workshop, tending to her butterflies and running her experiments, avoiding the town as much as she could.

After Welo died, when Wela was off in her thoughts, she would slip and say something like, "A strange land for a strange family" and "You've never tasted such sweetness as the Rodríguez pecans." A few days before she fell into the sleep, she said, "Mami once told me the story of her *abuelita*, who had so much of the gift in her. She could do the most amazing things with her mind: summon a flower to grow with a flick of her wrist or spark a fire with the snap of her fingers." Yolanda and Sonja knew better than to show interest and ask questions, because if they did, Wela would wave them off and shake her head. "Some other time, *mijas*."

But time seemed to be running out.

And Yolanda always wondered.

Why did their family have the gifts? Why Sonja?

Why not her?

She lifted her curls off her neck, letting the breeze cool her.

Pop. Click. Pop.

The blades of grass quivered in the breeze. Yolanda knelt and skimmed her fingers through the silky stalks, a sweet, fresh aroma settling in her nose and calming her. She took a deep breath, shivered, and gazed out to the silhouette of the pecan tree in the distance. There were so many questions Wela never answered. And now it might be too late.

How was she going to keep Wela out of hospice? How would she and Sonja avoid foster care? How was she going to make sure Rosalind Franklin didn't get taken away? The problems swirled in her mind, making her nauseous. It was all so hopeless. Her entire family was falling into a deep, dark hole, and no one was there to rescue them.

Yolanda walked up the steps and sat on the porch swing. She rifled through her backpack and found the gold journal. Wela's journal. The yellowed pages crinkled when she opened it to the bookmarked page, and a musty scent curled around her. She recognized Wela's slanted, scratchy handwriting, although it was much more precisely written than the shaky handwriting she now possessed.

September 17, 1942

Today the butterflies followed me to school again. I wasn't so sure last week, but now I know this is it.

This is my gift.

The orange-and-black ones like me best and follow me wherever I go. Cynthia trapped one in a cup at school last week and our teacher made her let it go outside. She called them black-veined brown butterflies. Another classmate said they were monarchs. I had to concentrate so hard I got a headache, but I was able to get them to stay outside today. Although, they can be quite distracting bouncing against the glass window in our classroom, waiting for me.

Mami says if I practice, I can learn how to control

them. She knew my gift was coming, of course, because she always knows things like that.

When I showed Violeta what I could do with the butterflies, she cried, which surprised me. She hoped the gift would skip me and leave me normal. She made me promise not to tell anyone outside of the family.

I promised.

The last thing I need is for Cynthia and Fiona to have another reason to ask me if I'm a bruja again. They call us the Rodríguez brujas. They've always called our family that. Even before Violeta did what she did. Mami says it's part of living here and part of who we are and that we shouldn't expect it to change.

Violeta's gift came when she was twelve too, and she hid it from everyone at school for as long as she could. But when Margaret Purty broke her arm and the bone was sticking out of the skin, that's when everyone found out about her. Violeta couldn't just leave her there writhing in pain.

She's spent the last four years trying to get everyone to forget. But once you see what Vi can do, there is no forgetting.

Raúl doesn't have one yet, but he's only ten. He thought it was really neat when I showed him the butterflies.

Mami tells us we are special and our gifts are to
be cherished. But I feel like being special makes us
outsiders. It's not only the children who whisper about
us. It's their parents too.

They remember when Mami's mama sold them
pecans from the orchard, so they still buy them from
us sometimes. But not without an odd glance or a
suspicious look.

And that word on their lips.

Bruja.

It's a powerful feeling when everyone is afraid of
you, but it's also lonely.

At least I have Vi.

We aren't brujas. At least, not the way they
mean it.

Yolanda closed the journal.

The light was beginning to fade, and the stars came out
one by one, announcing the arrival of night in the dusky
blue sky. A coyote howled in the distance. She closed her
eyes, thoughts of Wela in her mind.

Violeta. Wela had said her sister's name that morning.
She'd said, "*Lo siento.*" Wela was sorry about something. But
what was it?

Yolanda could relate to Wela's journal entry. It was

lonely to have an entire town saying those things about you. She realized that nothing much had changed in all the years since Wela had written that entry.

But to have a special skill—that would be incredible.

Her thoughts drifted again. What was going to happen to them? And why hadn't they heard from their dad? What was she going to do?

Rosalind Franklin barked in the distance, breaking her thoughts.

"Rosalind Franklin!" Yolanda yelled.

She barked again.

And again.

Yolanda jumped up and ran to the grass edge. The barking grew incessant and more urgent.

"Rosalind Franklin!"

Then Rosalind Franklin yelped.

"Come on, girl!" Yolanda frantically searched the grass for signs of movement, her heart pounding in her chest. There were none. "Rosalind Franklin!"

Silence.

There was a rustle in the grass, and Rosalind Franklin popped out and bolted for the back door.

A wave of relief washed over Yolanda. Thank goodness her dog was all right. She picked her up and let Rosalind Franklin lick her face, the dog's hot breath sticky and sweet from the grass. "You scared me, girl. I can't let anything happen to you."

She took Rosalind Franklin back inside and shut the door. The blue star flag hanging in the window was tangled up on itself from the wind. She fixed it, laying it flat against the glass, and checked the answering machine and her voice mail for any missed calls.

Nothing.

She padded into Wela's room and opened the windows to let the cool desert air in, the same way she would when Welo was sick. The popping grass echoed in the breeze.

Wela's breathing was quiet and restful. Yolanda tugged the yellow serape up under Wela's chin and bent down to kiss her cheek.

"Do you hear it, Wela? It's growing."

Nine

LATER that night, Yolanda woke drenched in sweat. The bedroom was hot and stuffy, but there was no way she could open the window. Hanging just outside, Sonja's bee house hummed faintly. Rosalind Franklin's black fur shone in the moonlight as she kneaded her paws against Yosemite. Sonja snored softly.

A voice called from downstairs.

Yolanda bolted upright. Her stomach lurched as she glanced over at Sonja, who was still asleep with the dogs curled around her. Some guard dogs. And Sonja could sleep through anything.

The voice called again.

"Yo-lan-da!"

Who was that? She held her breath and waited. Her heart pounded so loudly in her ears, she wasn't sure she could hear anything at all.

Then she stood, the floorboards creaking beneath her feet. She tiptoed to the bedroom door and listened.

Nothing.

She opened the door and snuck out into the dark hall, her feet tangling on the straps of one of Sonja's hiking backpacks. She tripped and hit the ground with a *thud*, her knee slamming into the wood floor.

Sonja! Why did she insist on packing for a camping trip when Dad was halfway across the world?

Yolanda stood up and looked back into the bedroom. Rosalind Franklin's head snapped up, and Yolanda pressed her fingers to her lips. Sonja grumbled and rolled over, and Yosemite snuggled deep into the covers. Sliding the backpacks across the floor to the other side of the hall, Yolanda crept to the top of the stairs and waited.

Nothing.

"Yo-lan-da!" the voice called again.

Rosalind Franklin popped off the bed and scampered over to Yolanda's feet.

She heard the back door open and the screen slam shut.

Rosalind Franklin growled, and the hackles on her back stood on end. Yolanda swallowed hard, picked up Rosalind Franklin, and crept down the stairs, each step creaking under her feet. She searched the darkened hallway, but there was no one there. She padded quietly to Wela's bedroom and peeked through the crack in the door.

The covers were disheveled. Wela's bed was empty.

A surge of excitement ripped through her. Where was she? Was Wela awake?

Her heart raced as she tiptoed through the kitchen and into the living room.

There was no one there.

The heavy wooden door to the back porch creaked in the hot wind. It was open.

Yolanda looked out the window, and there she was.

Wela.

Yolanda almost shouted her name in excitement, but she held it in. Was this really happening? Was this real?

Wela's long white hair was disheveled, and the colorful embroidered nightgown pooled around her ankles. She was sitting on the steps, drinking a glass of orange juice. The yellow serape from her bed was wrapped over her shoulders while the butterflies opened and closed their wings in the white curls down her back.

It was her. It was Wela and she was awake. Yolanda's

heart pounded in her ears. "Wela?" She quietly opened the screen door.

Wela smiled, set the glass on the step, and patted the space next to her. *"Siéntate, mija."*

With Wela's voice, Yolanda's heart leapt and Rosalind Franklin wiggled in her arms.

"You're okay! You're awake!" She put Rosalind Franklin down, ran to Wela, and threw her arms around her. "I'm so sorry for what I said, the argument and everything. I didn't mean it."

She squeezed Wela so tight, she didn't want to ever let go. Now everything would be fine. Wela would be able to keep them all together—as a family. Everything was going to be okay.

"I have so much to tell you. They wanted to send me and Sonja to a foster home, but now that you are awake— we haven't heard from Dad yet— Oh! And my science fair project was a complete disaster—and there's this weird grass that started growing out there."

She embraced Wela again, hugging her for a long time. She rubbed the embroidered flowers on Wela's night-gown with her thumb, and Wela's curls tickled her nose, but Yolanda wasn't going to let go. A butterfly bounced from curl to curl in the dim light. It almost seemed as if it would fall, but it would gracefully catch itself on another curl. Something wasn't right. Wela was quiet. Too quiet. Yolanda pulled away.

Wela was frowning. "I don't have long, *mija*."

"What do you mean?"

"I don't have much time."

"Much time for what?"

"To get there," Wela said, her breath escaping her. She paused for a moment. "I need you to take me to the pecan tree."

"The pecan tree?" Yolanda looked into the black night. There was moonlight, but it was too dark to see all the way to the tree. "What for?"

"Oh, *mija*. It's calling me." Wela's voice caught and her eyes glistened. "I'm dying." Wela's expression changed from sadness to determination. "We have to find it before it's too late."

The excitement from seeing Wela now dissolved into nothing, and the pit of worry invaded Yolanda's gut again. She was dying? Something wasn't right. What was she talking about? "Find what?"

"*La caja. La caja. La caja.*" Wela repeated the words over and over again and stood, running her fingers through her hair and disturbing the butterflies. "I know he put it here somewhere."

"A box? You're looking for a box?" Yolanda placed her

hand on Wela's shoulder to calm her, but it was no use. Wela kept pacing.

"What kind of box? How big is it?"

Wela snapped. "It's the box! I have to find the box!" Her shoulders slumped and she hung her head. She leaned against the wall and pushed her palms against her eyes.

Yolanda hated to see Wela upset like this. What if it caused her to go back into the sleep? "I'll help you. We'll find it. Don't worry." She took Wela's arm and guided her to the swing on the porch. Rosalind Franklin jumped up on the swing and sat between them.

Wela patted her head and raised an eyebrow. "You little *maldita bonita*, you've been a bad girl, haven't you, eating my *chanclas*?" Rosalind Franklin nuzzled her head into Wela's hand and licked it once before resting her head on Wela's lap.

"You falling into the sleep was my fault, wasn't it?" Yolanda tapped her toes together, searching the ground for answers.

"Oh no, no, no." Wela wrapped an arm around her and hugged her close. "It's not."

"I should have never said those things. I'm really sorry."

"I know you are," Wela said. "But you know, as much as I don't want to admit it, there was truth to what you said."

Yolanda glanced up, surprised to hear Wela say that. "Really?"

"We all have our reasons for doing the things we do. I hope one day, even if you don't agree with me, you will understand why I did it."

She would never understand why Wela would burn all of Welo's notes. It was cruel to throw away his life's work like that. How could she? "I just don't understand why you would destr—" She stopped herself. Not now. She gripped Wela's hand.

"Promise you will take me. *Mañana*. Tomorrow."

"I will. Of course I will." Yolanda gripped Wela's hands in hers. "It will make you better, won't it? That's what you always say—it's a strange land."

Wela didn't say anything for a moment, as though she was considering her answer. "Something like that." She patted the tops of Yolanda's hands. "What I know for certain is everything will be set right when we get there." Wela pressed her lips together. "I hope."

That was good enough for her. If Wela said everything was going to be all right, then it was. Yolanda rested her head on Wela's shoulder. "If it will make you better, I'll take you anywhere. We'll look for the box first thing in the morning."

It was nice to have this time alone with Wela. Without Sonja needing something. Wela brushed a curl from her cheek and tucked it behind her ear. "You remind me so much of your *mamá*. You have so much of her in you."

She melted into Wela's arms. Wela didn't talk about Mamá often. Once Welo told her it was too painful. It was too painful for both of them.

Wela pulled her in close, so warm and secure. The swing creaked back and forth.

Pop. Click. Pop.

"Do you hear that?" Yolanda whispered, looking up at Wela's wrinkled face.

Wela nodded. "*Está creciendo.*"

Yolanda didn't know what that meant.

"'*Crecer*' means 'to grow'—it's growing."

"But why?"

"It's a strange land, *mija*. For generations, our family has lived here on this land. When I was a little girl, it was a pecan orchard, and me and my family used to sell pecans to the townsfolk here. They were the sweetest, most delicious pecans anyone had ever tasted."

Yolanda laid her head in Wela's lap and Wela began her story.

Ten

"**STAND UP** straight, Jo," Mami said, pouring the hard round nuts into canvas sacks. Violeta scooped large handfuls of nuts into crates while Raúl unloaded more empty crates from the trailer. "You need to look approachable or no one will buy from us."

This was before I knew about my gift with the butterflies, and I was being my usual stubborn self. It was a beautiful clear Sunday in early September, the beginning of the harvest season, and we had set up our tent across from the church. The road was empty, except for us and our table of pecans. I would have rather been anywhere else than in front of the church, and I'm pretty sure my brother and sister would have agreed with me. At eleven o'clock on the dot, right when the church bells rang, the double doors opened and the churchgoers with their clean faces and pastel dresses poured out.

A butterfly landed on my forearm. I raised it to eye level. The sunlight shone through its thin, papery wings. The black lines looked as though they had been drawn on with charcoal, letting no light through.

"Josefa! Pay attention!" Mami scolded.

I gently shook off the butterfly, and it flew haphazardly from underneath our tent.

"Mami, why are we even here? These church folks won't buy from us," Violeta said. It had been four years of poor sales, and Mami was determined to change that this year. Violeta blamed herself, of course, ever since that day on the playground with Margaret Purty, the rumors were rampant about what she'd done. That's when people stopped buying from us.

"Because if you can get their leader, you can get the rest of them to follow," Mami whispered, peering through the crowd. "And I had a dream last night . . . a dream Pastor Jones was thinking about our pecans."

Mami was always having dreams, thoughts like that.

The parishioners walked by our stand, many not even tipping a hat to say hello.

"Some church folks," I muttered.

"Jo," Mami warned. "They are only afraid of what they do

not understand. If you smiled and stood up straight, maybe they would say hello."

Pastor Jones spotted us from the steps. He continued to shake a few hands, but it was obvious from his craning neck he couldn't resist.

Mami waved to him, and he lifted his hat.

"You see—I told you," Mami said under her breath. "Buenos días, Pastor Jones!" She waved.

"Señora Rodríguez, what do we have here?" Pastor Jones bellowed, rubbing his fat belly. His voice was so deep and loud, you felt it rattle your soul when he spoke. That's what Cynthia Purty told me once, and I couldn't help but agree. Fiona Jones, his daughter, and Cynthia Purty's best friend, peered out from behind him, her stringy blond hair hanging on either side of her face.

"Would you like to try one?" I offered a nut to Pastor Jones, and he took it in his chubby fingers.

"They are the world-famous Rodríguez pecans. Sweetest ones you'll ever taste." I offered one to Fiona, who stared at me with cold eyes. She shook her head and darted behind her father.

"Fiona is a bit on the shy side," Pastor Jones said. He placed the nut in his mouth, chewed, and shook his head. "My, oh my, do I love those pecans. I've missed them. I'll take a crate this year."

"Wonderful," Mami said, smiling. She shot Raúl a look. He grabbed a full crate from the trailer and set it on the table.

Pastor Jones dipped his hand into the sample bowl, spilling a few on the table. He shook them in his palm before throwing them back in his mouth. "You know, Señora Rodríguez, we'd love it if you and your family would join our congregation. You seem like such good people. I know you'd probably get more business if people got to know you and your family a little better." Pastor Jones raised an eyebrow. A chewed bit of pecan hung from his lower lip.

"Gracias, Pastor Jones." Mami nodded. "But my family has been here longer than—" Mami stopped herself, wiping her hands on her apron and smiling. She pushed the crate across the table.

"You are just in need of the Lord—"

"Gracias, Pastor Jones." Mami's eyes crinkled so hard from the fake smile it was almost a scowl.

Pastor Jones shook his head, took his crate, and left, Fiona trailing behind.

After Pastor Jones left, the townsfolk lined up to buy their pecans. With his purchase, it was as though we had suddenly been thrust into the light. Cynthia and Margaret Purty stood in line with their mother.

"Buenos días," Mami said. "What would you like today?"

"We'll take the same as the pastor." Mrs. Purty nodded toward the pile of crates.

Violeta began to scoop nuts into an empty crate.

"Mother." Margaret rubbed a silver scar on her forearm. "I won't eat them if she touches them." She pointed right at Violeta and mouthed the word "bruja."

The color drained from Violeta's face.

"Margaret." Mrs. Purty laughed nervously and pushed her daughter's hand away. "Enough of that."

"Would you like a sample?" I held a nut out for Cynthia. She sat two rows behind me in school and was usually nice, even though she liked to ask me if I was a bruja every now and then. Cynthia nodded, took it from my palm, and placed it in her mouth.

I offered one to Margaret. She shook her head.

"They are really good, Margaret," Cynthia said.

Violeta filled the crate and Mrs. Purty paid Mami. Just as they were about to leave, Margaret glanced back and said, "Okay—fine, I'll try one."

I smiled, so sweetly, and plucked the nut out of the shell, leaving only the corky bitter part. Raúl shot me a look and then busied himself with a bag on the table. I placed the shell in Margaret's palm and whispered in her ear, "This is my favorite part."

For a split second I almost felt bad. Almost. But then she turned, glared at Violeta, and popped a corky piece in her mouth.

Her face slackened as she chewed. Margaret spit the bitter part into her hand and threw it on the ground.

I covered my mouth to stifle a giggle.

"Josefa!" Mami snapped.

Raúl and Violeta giggled too. Mrs. Purty hadn't noticed, but Cynthia winked at me as Margaret clawed at her tongue.

Eleven

THE NEXT morning, a loud roaring sound woke Yolanda. She was warm, wrapped in the yellow serape, but her back ached from sleeping on the hard swing.

She was alone.

Wela was gone. Yolanda sat up and looked around. Hasik was cutting the grass with a weed trimmer, flinging long blades all over the place. It had grown even taller overnight.

She squinted. The grass towered over his head.

How strange. How had it grown so quickly?

She stood and saw the grass went as far as she could see. Now that it was daylight, she could see the lone pecan tree, standing there on top of the butte.

Had it been a dream?

She spotted the empty orange juice glass on the step. It couldn't have been a dream. She raced inside toward Wela's bedroom, trailing the serape behind her. Mrs. Patel was in the kitchen burning scrambled eggs.

"Good morning, Yolanda. Isn't that grass so odd? I asked Hasik to come trim it down a bit."

"Is she awake?" Yolanda didn't wait for her answer and slid into the bedroom, her heart racing in her chest.

Her heart sank.

There was Wela, the sheets pulled up to her armpits, asleep. Yolanda walked over to the bed and placed a hand over Wela's rising chest. Her heart thumped lightly under Yolanda's hand. It was as though Wela had never moved.

Tears pricked Yolanda's eyes. It couldn't have been a dream. It had felt so real. She needed it to be real.

Wela was dying.

"I'm sorry you girls have had to go through all of this." Mrs. Patel stood in the doorway holding an egg-covered spatula. "I spoke with Abby, and she told me the plan."

Yolanda glanced up.

"They are coming at two o'clock to pick Josefa up, and then you and Sonja are going with Abby." Mrs. Patel hung her head. "I'm so sorry."

Yolanda shut her eyes and shook her head. This couldn't

be happening. Wela was fine last night. Yolanda placed a finger in Wela's hair and let a butterfly climb onto it.

"Yolanda?"

"Fine," she said without looking up. It wasn't fine. But what was she supposed to do? Scream and cry? Throw a fit? She was too old for that now.

"You girls have had to grow up so much in the last year." Mrs. Patel lingered in the doorway. "I wish Amar and I could care for you girls, but I haven't been back to India since I lost my mother and I want to be there when my little sister gets married."

Yolanda forced the words out, even though she didn't mean them. "It's okay, Mrs. Patel. I understand." Abandonment was a Patel specialty. First Ghita, now her mother.

"I'm going to the grocery store later. Is there anything you need me to pick up before they come?"

Yolanda's head snapped up. "Yes. My epinephrine. I need it refilled."

"I will take care of that for you."

"Thanks." Her thoughts swirled about the conversation she'd had with Wela the night before. The tree. She had to take Wela to the tree. Everything would be set right if she could just get her to the tree.

No matter what.

The tree would save her.

Mrs. Patel lingered in the doorway.

"The *huevos* are burning," Yolanda said, glancing over her shoulder.

"Right-o." Mrs. Patel flicked the spatula before shuffling off to the kitchen.

Twelve

AFTER Mrs. Patel left for the grocery store, Yolanda spent the next few hours searching the house for the box. She wished Wela had told her more about it. Was it made of wood? Metal? How big was it? She looked in all the closets and cabinets and under the beds, but nothing turned up that could be what Wela was looking for. They were all boxes filled with old, forgotten items. Old clothing, books. Nothing that contained anything that would cause Wela so much angst.

Yolanda and Rosalind Franklin made their way to the workshop. She found dusty old boxes of microscope slides, piles of textbooks, and an old butterfly cage. Deep in the back of the shelves, she uncovered a book of old photographs. As she flipped through the yellowed pages, she recognized a picture of Welo, Wela, and Mamá. Welo's flop of dark hair peeked from underneath his cowboy hat, and Wela's butterflies adorned her dark curls. Neither Welo nor Wela was smiling. Welo's lips were pressed into a thin line as his eyes stared right at the camera, and Wela was looking off in the distance, seemingly lost in her thoughts. Mamá, who must have been about twelve, was smiling. A great big smile that caught Yolanda's breath. She thought for a moment that she was looking at a picture of herself. They looked alike, their matching dark curls, their brown skin. The way their noses scrunched up when they smiled. Although Yolanda didn't smile much lately. It was startling at first and then comforting to see her own face reflected in her mother's. She'd been so used to Sonja and her dad's looks being compared that at times she felt like she wasn't even part of their family. But now, seeing her likeness in Mamá made her remember a piece of where she came from. Yolanda tucked the photograph back in the book and placed it on the shelf. She sat back on her heels and bit her lip. The box Wela was looking for wasn't in the house or in the workshop.

She didn't have much time to waste. It was nearly one o'clock. She'd spent hours looking for the box only to come up empty-handed. She hoped that whatever was in it wasn't that important. She and Rosalind Franklin went outside. If she was going to take Wela to the tree, she had a lot to do.

She needed to find Hasik. She was going to have to convince him of something. Something he might not believe.

Ghita and Sonja were lounging on the porch swing with Yosemite between them, their heads resting against each other, the bees orbiting the space over them. Ghita's eyes were red and puffy, as though she'd been crying, and Sonja ran her finger along the soft spot on Yosemite's nose. Neither looked up when Yolanda passed by.

Yolanda and Rosalind Franklin bounced down the steps to the large rectangle of grass. Hasik had cut down an area the size of a small yard and was loading the cut grass into large garbage bags and setting them on the side of the house. The tall grass continued on behind him. Her gaze lingered on the pecan tree. Even in the hazy distance she figured, it couldn't be that far.

When Hasik saw her, he stood up straight and pushed the flecks of grass out of his sweaty face with the back of his hand. "Hey."

She caught herself staring at his white smile shining in the sunlight. She blushed and looked away.

Rosalind Franklin darted in the grass after a lizard.

"Rosalind Franklin, get back here!" Yolanda was

worried about her getting lost in the grass again. Rosalind Franklin popped out from the grass, grunting and snorting, and ran to Hasik. She licked at the bits of green grass on his legs.

He bent down to pet her. "I'm sorry about . . . well, everything. When we get back from our trip, I'll take care of your dogs. Do you know what you are going to do with them?"

Yolanda hadn't even thought about it. There was no point, since she wasn't going to let them be taken away. "I'm certainly not surrendering her. And no one in this town talks to us except you guys." She shielded her eyes from the bright sun. She could still hear the pops and clicks from the grass. "Why are you cutting the grass anyway?"

Hasik admired his handiwork. "My mom figured maybe you guys can enjoy it when you come back. When your dad comes back and you are a family again."

"Who knows if he'll ever come back." They walked to the stairs and sat on the bottom step. "You've heard the stories. Soldier on his fourth tour killed by an exploded bomb or an ambush or—whatever. It's hard to stay optimistic after all this time. And even if he does come back, he'll just want to leave us again."

"You don't know that." Hasik's eyes softened.

"Sure I do." It was sweet that Hasik thought her dad

would stick around, but she wasn't going to hold out hope anymore. If he wanted to leave them, then that was his choice. Her priority was getting Wela better.

Hasik glanced back at the swing. "She's pretty upset about this—Ghita. She doesn't want to see you guys taken away."

Yolanda glanced over her shoulder. "She doesn't want to see *Sonja* taken away. She could care less about anyone else." When Hasik didn't say anything after that she knew she had to be right. Ghita cared about only two things: Ghita. And Sonja. That had been clear since last fall.

Yolanda picked up a stick, dug at the dusty earth, and chewed her bottom lip. "Do you think it's possible for someone like Wela to wake up and then go back to sleep?"

"I don't know. . . . What did the doctors say?"

"They said there is no medical explanation for her to be like this."

Hasik shrugged. "I guess anything is possible."

"I agree." Yolanda stuck the stick in the ground and it broke. "Anything *is* possible—I'm just having a hard time wrapping my mind around it."

"Around what?"

Yolanda lowered her eyes and whispered, "Wela woke up last night. I talked to her."

Hasik laughed nervously. "What? Yo, that's crazy. I saw

her in bed this morning. She was the same as she has been for weeks."

"I swear. I talked to her last night. She asked me to take her to the pecan tree. She said it would cure her and make her better. She and I have had our problems, but one thing I know for certain: She doesn't lie." Yolanda stood, walked around in a circle with her hands on her hips, and pointed her finger like Wela would. "*No mentiras*, she always says."

Hasik stood and wiped his palms on his jeans. He brushed his hair back from his sweaty forehead. "I know this is a stressful situation. You have a lot going on, but maybe you had a dream."

She could tell by the look on his face he didn't believe her. "She talked to me, Hasik. It wasn't a dream! She made me promise."

Sonja popped her head over the porch railing. "What are you guys talking about?"

"Nothing," Yolanda mumbled. The last thing she needed was Sonja getting involved. She lowered her voice. "Wela never asks me to do anything for her. I have to do this."

"Yolan—" Hasik shifted his weight and avoided her gaze.

Yolanda stepped in front of him and made him look at her. "Please," she pleaded. "I can't do this without you. I need your help."

Hasik sighed, glanced at the tree, and rubbed the back of his neck. "Even if we do this, how in the world are we going to get her there? She's asleep."

Yolanda pointed at the wheelbarrow, and Hasik laughed. "That is so not going to work."

"Sure it is. We can lift her in it together. Wheel it next to the porch and wait for me there."

"Yo—"

"Just do it!"

Thirteen

YOLANDA bolted upstairs to her and Sonja's room. She rummaged through Sonja's nightstand, looking for the music box with the twirling ballerina. Wela had given them matching pink music boxes for their eighth birthdays. Sonja had covered hers with flag stickers Dad brought from the countries he had traveled to. South Korea, Germany, Afghanistan, Iraq. There was hardly any pink showing anymore. She opened the top and bent the spring holding the ballerina to keep the music from playing. Yolanda hadn't seen the original ballerina in a long time. With a black marker, Sonja had drawn tall hiking boots to cover up the ballet slippers and a vest and shorts over the pink leotard and tutu.

She lifted the pink velvet insert, and there it was. Mamá's compass.

A shiny silver circle bound in rich red leather. It was heavier than she remembered, fitting in the center of her palm. Dad had given it to Mamá after they returned from their first tour of Afghanistan. She was a medic and had saved his life when he was nearly killed by a roadside bomb.

Dad had given it to Sonja after she showed interest in the outdoors. They bonded over camping and hiking. Yolanda had been jealous, but she'd never said anything, of course. That was how it was for as long as she could remember. When he was home, Dad and Sonja were always together.

Yolanda didn't own anything of Mamá's. And she certainly didn't know how to use a compass. But maybe Hasik did. She replaced the insert, closed the box, and set it back in the nightstand.

Next she went over to the camping backpacks. Sonja had already packed for her and Dad, and she assumed they contained most of what she would need inside.

Yolanda slung the red one over her shoulder and shoved the compass deep in the bottom of the blue one, just as Sonja and Ghita walked in.

"What are you doing?" Sonja's hands were on her hips, her eyes narrowed. The bees flew around her head.

"Nothing," Yolanda mumbled, and started to leave.

"Those are mine!" Sonja grabbed the blue backpack and tried to wrestle it away, but Yolanda held on to the strap.

"I need it."

"For what? Camping?" Sonja scoffed. The bees danced around her head and sped up, almost angrily. Yolanda ducked, but held on.

"No, for something else."

"Get it later." Ghita gently touched Sonja's arm. "I need to talk to you." Sonja glared at Yolanda but let go of the backpack. Yolanda used the opportunity to push past the girls, run down the stairs, and slide into Wela's bedroom.

She was still tucked in bed, her chest rising with each breath, her eyes closed.

"Wela, wake up." Yolanda shook her, but Wela didn't move. "Please wake up!" The butterflies opened and closed their wings in her hair. "I know you can hear me. We're running out of time." Yolanda glanced at her phone. It was 1:45 p.m.

She left the bedroom and entered the kitchen. Foraging through the refrigerator, she found leftover tamales, naan, and a few bananas. She filled the empty water bottles and stuck them in the sides of the backpack. She popped her head out the window to see Hasik standing next to the porch with the wheelbarrow, just as she'd asked. She zipped up the backpacks and opened the back door.

"Here, take these." Yolanda tossed the packs across the porch.

Hasik shook his head, but he picked up the blue one and then the red and set them next to the stairs. "This is crazy."

Yolanda ignored him. "I'll be right back." She darted back inside.

"Sonja! Talk to me." Ghita grasped Sonja by the arms. They stood near the front door and didn't see Yolanda. She ducked behind the wall and peeked around the corner.

"No. I can't. I can't do this." Sonja pushed Ghita away.

"Please, please don't," Ghita pleaded.

A white van pulled up and parked in the front of the house, its brakes squealing as it stopped. On the side, in blue letters, it said MEITNER PLACE. Yolanda pulled out her phone. It was 1:55 p.m. Abby would be here any minute.

Yolanda crept into the bedroom. Wela still hadn't moved.

"Wake up!" Yolanda shook her by the shoulders. The butterflies flew away for a moment and then settled back in her hair. This was hopeless. "They're here," Yolanda said quietly.

Wela still didn't wake.

The ruby-colored sedan pulled into the driveway and Abby stepped out of the car.

Yolanda rushed to the back porch. "Hasik, hurry. Come inside."

"Do I need to bring the wheelbarrow?"

"No. Come on!" Yolanda ran back inside the house. "Hurry!"

Sonja and Ghita stood in the doorway facing each other, lost in their own world, unaware of all that was happening around them. The bees flew faster and faster, in a hazy blur above their heads. Ghita touched Sonja's cheek and leaned in. Sonja closed her eyes.

And then they kissed.

Yolanda sucked in a sharp breath.

The bees froze in midair above their heads for a split second, even though it felt like an eternity.

Then the doorbell rang.

Fourteen

AS GHITA and Sonja parted, Sonja opened her eyes and smiled at Ghita. "See?" Ghita said.

Yolanda's hand flew to her mouth. She knew there was something going on between them, but seeing it was somehow a shock. She knew she should move, but she couldn't. She was frozen.

The bees, drunk from the kiss, flew around their heads drowsily. Sonja glanced over, her eyes meeting Yolanda's. Sonja's cheeks flushed, and her lips parted in surprise.

Yolanda wasn't supposed to see that. But it seemed that everyone knew already. It wasn't a secret.

It wasn't a secret—anymore.

Yolanda ran down the hall.

"Yo!" Sonja called after her. Yolanda darted into Wela's bedroom and slammed the door, her heart pounding. She hadn't expected to see them kiss. And it didn't look like it was the first time.

"*Mija*," a voice muttered. Yolanda looked up.

Wela sat on the edge of the bed, bright-eyed, her feet hovering over the floor. Yolanda ran to Wela, her arms wide. "You're awake!" Yolanda threw her arms around her. It hadn't been a dream after all.

"We have to hurry," Yolanda said.

"My *chanclas*, *mija*." Wela pointed to the vanity. She placed her index finger on the pillow, letting one of her butterflies crawl onto it. Then she placed the butterfly, its wings opening and closing, into her hair.

Yolanda slipped the brown leather *chanclas* onto Wela's feet. "Aye, Rosalind Franklin—" Wela raised an eyebrow at Yolanda. She'd noticed the teeth marks in the leather. Yolanda gave her sheepish grin.

Just then the bedroom door opened. "Mrs. Rodríguez, you're awake. How wonder—" Hasik started to say as he looked at Yolanda. She shot him a *see? I told you* look.

"*Ven aquí*, come here and help me, *por favor*." Wela reached for his arm. He dove under an elbow and helped her stand, her embroidered nightgown flouncing at her feet.

"My mother will be so happy to see you," he said.

Wela, even though she was much smaller than Hasik's towering frame, righted herself and looked him in the eyes. "*Mijito*, we aren't telling your mother anything." Wela pressed her lips into a thin, stubborn line and placed her hands firmly on his shoulders. "*Nada*. You hear me? Nothing." She gently tapped his cheek with her palm twice.

Hasik nodded, his eyes wide. There was no arguing with Wela normally. But especially not a Wela who just miraculously woke up from an unexplained sleep.

"Take me outside," she said, flicking her hand toward the ceiling. "*¡Vámonos!*"

The doorbell rang again as they entered the hallway to the kitchen. There were two men in white scrubs, waiting. The tall one peered through the side window. Abby was walking up the driveway when Mrs. Patel pulled up in her silver sedan.

Yolanda dashed back into the bedroom, grabbed the yellow serape from Wela's bed, and covered Wela's head and shoulders.

"*La caja, mija*. Did you find the box?" Wela asked.

Yolanda's shoulders fell in defeat. "I searched everywhere, the whole house, the workshop, but I couldn't find it." A thought occurred to her. The *casita*. "Could it be at the *casita*? I know Welo used to do his research there."

He had mentioned the *casita* that day when his eyes were wild and he made Yolanda promise to take Wela to the tree. Maybe that was what he was talking about.

Wela tapped her lip and nodded. "I bet you are right, *mija*. That's where he took a lot of his work that I did not approve of." She stared down her nose. "We'll have to stop there on the way to the tree."

"Take her to the edge of the grass, through the back. I'll meet you there," she told Hasik. He nodded and helped Wela through the kitchen and out the back door.

Once Yolanda was sure she heard the back door close, she opened the front door.

"Hello," the taller man said. "My name is Adam. I'm with Meitner Place, and we are here to pick up"—he glanced at his clipboard—"a Josefa Rodríguez."

They had to consult their clipboard for her name. Yolanda was even more sure about what she was going to do now. She nodded solemnly and opened the door wider to let them in. Sonja rounded the corner, Ghita following her.

"Sonja, I'm sorry, but I—"

"Stop!" Sonja held up a hand. "I'm not talking about this now—I need to say goodbye to Wela."

Out of the corner of her eye, Yolanda glanced at Sonja, who refused to look at her. Sonja pressed her lips together, but Yolanda could see her chin quivering and the tears shining in her eyes. Ghita nodded and sat down on the bottom of the steps, burying her head in her hands. Yolanda felt a pull to console Ghita, wrap an arm around her and tell her everything was going to be okay, but she stopped herself.

They weren't friends anymore.

Yolanda led the two men to the living room. "It'll be a few minutes. If you could wait here, we'd like to say good-bye."

The men sat down. Yolanda grabbed Sonja's hand and pulled her into Wela's bedroom, closing the door behind them.

She heard Mrs. Patel come in through the front door. "Girls, Abby is here too," she called.

"Wait! Where's We—" Sonja said.

Yolanda placed a finger to her lips and waited until she heard Mrs. Patel and Abby greeting the men in the living room.

"Where is she?" Sonja demanded, her voice growing loud. "What is going on?" Yolanda placed her hand over Sonja's mouth. Sonja tried to fight her off, but Yolanda held on tight, sneaking her through the bathroom, through the kitchen, and out the back door before finally letting her go.

Sonja glared at her, her blue eyes blazing. "Where is she?"

Yolanda pointed. Hasik and Wela stood in the freshly mowed lawn, the yellow serape draped over her shoulders.

Wela waved, and Sonja's mouth fell open.

"I'm taking her to the pecan tree. She asked me to. It's the only way to save her."

"What are you talking about?" Sonja said. "Are you crazy? You'll never make it." Her eyes narrowed. "*She'll* never make it."

"We'll manage. Keep an eye on Rosalind Franklin for me?" Yolanda bounced down the steps, grabbed the red backpack, and slung it over her shoulder. The house phone rang, echoing through the open door.

Yolanda hesitated. No one called the house phone except for one person.

Dad.

She started back toward the phone and then stopped herself. Ghita, Mrs. Patel, and Abby were coming through the kitchen toward the back door. She locked eyes with Sonja.

Please, Yolanda mouthed.

"No." Sonja crossed her arms.

"It could be Dad." Yolanda tightened the strap over her shoulder as the wave of realization washed over Sonja's face.

As Sonja bolted inside, Yolanda jogged to Wela and Hasik. The blue backpack was inside the wheelbarrow and

Hasik had pushed it across the lawn to the edge of the tall grass. Wela stood on shaky legs, her face bright and eager.

"Ready?" Yolanda asked.

"Are you sure about this?" Hasik glanced back at Wela and Yolanda, not looking sure himself.

"Are you sure, Wela?" Yolanda gripped Wela's frail hand tight in hers.

"*Vámonos.*"

The sun, high in the sky and hot, beat over them. Towering over their heads, the grass, blades thin and green, popped and clicked.

Yolanda took one last look at the big white house with the wraparound porch. The blue star on the red-and-white flag shimmered in the sunlight.

She parted the popping blades with the back of her hand and pulled Wela behind her, leading the way into the cool darkness of the tall, tall grass.

Fifteen

THE GRASS snapped shut behind them, and it was quiet.

Too quiet. As though the world Yolanda left behind had never, ever been. It was disorienting and calming at the same time. They had made it.

A voice called out in the distance. Yolanda ducked in the towering grass. There was no telling if anyone could see where they were from the porch, even if she couldn't see them. The fresh sweet scent of the grass tickled her nose.

She heard a faint jingle.

Yolanda started walking, pulling Wela behind her as Hasik pushed the wheelbarrow. The grass was thick and difficult to navigate. Yolanda had to concentrate as her feet tangled on the grass and the blades hit her in the face. She couldn't see more than a few feet in front of her. Wela stumbled behind her. This was going to take much longer than she had thought. They needed to find their way to the *casita* first, and Yolanda had only a vague idea of where it was. It was also impossible to see which direction they were heading with the grass towering over them.

Suddenly, a voice spoke.

"I thought you were going to leave without me."

Yolanda spun around, and her shoulders sagged in disappointment.

Sonja.

Of course Sonja had come. She always had to find a way to be involved in everything.

Sonja emerged from the dense grass, a hiking backpack slung over her shoulder. Out popped Rosalind Franklin, her dog tags tinkling.

"Go back. We can manage just fine without you—thanks." Yolanda turned around and started to pull Wela behind her again. Having Sonja and Rosalind Franklin come along was only going to be a hindrance. "Besides, don't you have *other* things to deal with?" Yolanda muttered under her breath.

Sonja bolted ahead of the group and stopped, blocking their way. "Oh, come on. You need me." Sonja dug into her pack and pulled out a pair of machetes. "Look, I brought these. You're going to need them if you want to get through this." She swiped the machete back and forth in front of her, slicing the grass down and cutting a clear path.

Yolanda stared at her sister. Of course she thought of the machetes. She thought of everything.

Wela suddenly paled and her knees gave out.

"Wela!" Yolanda caught her before gently laying her on the ground and kneeling beside her.

"I'm okay, just feeling a little faint." Her wrinkled skin was greenish, her lips cracked and dry.

Yolanda unscrewed the top of a water bottle and placed it to Wela's lips.

She took a sip. "That's better, *mija*. Thank you."

"She'll never make it," another voice said.

Yolanda glanced up.

Ghita.

Ghita stood with her arms crossed over her chest, looking quite sure of herself. "You have to take her back."

Yolanda groaned. What was she doing here? This was starting to fall apart. She definitely didn't want Sonja and Ghita coming along. They would only complicate things. They needed to go back.

"What are you doing here?" Sonja said. "I told you I don't want to do this right now."

"You have to go back." Ghita pushed her long dark hair from her face. "Wela can't stay out here. Look at her—she's sick."

Wela pushed herself up on her elbows and looked Ghita square in the eyes. "I am not going back." Her voice was stern and clear. "We are going to the tree."

Ghita's gaze shifted down as she kicked at the ground with the tip of her shoe. "Well, I'm not going to be a part of this."

"No one asked you to!" Yolanda snapped. "Just go." She helped Wela drink another sip of water.

"Go back," Sonja said.

Ghita didn't move. She instead stared at Hasik.

Sonja placed her hands on her hips. "Go."

Ghita ignored her. "Amma is going to be really angry if you don't come back with me, Hasik." Ghita tapped her foot. "You're being a *majnu*."

Hasik rubbed the back of his neck. "Mom won't be mad," he said, but his voice didn't sound so sure. "And don't call me that." His grip tightened on the wheelbarrow handles.

Yolanda didn't want Ghita to stay, and she certainly didn't expect her to. It was Ghita after all. Abandoner-in-chief. But she wasn't going to let her convince Hasik to leave.

"What does that mean, Ghita? *Majnu*?"

Ghita raised her eyebrows and nodded toward Hasik. "I'll let him tell you."

"It's nothing," Hasik said, but his face said something different. "She's trying to embarrass me."

"Yeah, she's good at that," Sonja muttered.

A hurt looked crossed Ghita's face.

They must be fighting, Yolanda thought. The realization didn't bring her as much satisfaction as she thought it would. Wela reached for the water bottle, and Yolanda gave her another sip. Then she screwed the cap on the bottle. They needed to go.

Yolanda climbed to her feet. "We don't have time for this. We need to get going. So, Ghita, you head back to the house and let us get on our way."

"Fine," Ghita said, raising her arms in defeat.

Good. This was better. Ghita was leaving without a fight. Now, if Yolanda could just get Sonja to go with her.

Ghita spun around in a circle. "Do you know which way the house is?"

The grass towered over Yolanda's head, making it impossible to tell which direction they'd come from. She turned around, the never-ending grass blurring all around her.

"The house is that way. Behind us." Yolanda pointed and then hesitated, biting her lip. "Or maybe it's that way."

Sonja sighed and dropped her backpack to the ground.

"I couldn't find my compass," she said. "So I can't be sure, unless I look."

Yolanda's gut squeezed with guilt as the compass weighed extra heavy in her pack. But she wasn't going to tell Sonja she had it. This was not the right time for a fight.

"The pecan tree is directly south of the house," Sonja said. "I'll need to climb on someone's shoulders to see over the grass."

Sonja scrambled onto Hasik's shoulders and he winced as her sneakers dug into his back. Rosalind Franklin barked and jumped up and down.

"Enough, girl," Yolanda said, picking her up. "We need to get to the *casita* first. See if you can spot it."

Sonja's long red braids hung down either shoulder, the bees darting in and out of her hair. Shielding her eyes from the bright sun, she looked one way and then the other. "Hmm, the pecan tree is that way." She pointed the same direction Yolanda had pointed. "The *casita* is over there, but the house . . . is gone."

"What?" Ghita said. "What do you mean?"

Sonja scoured the horizon. "I mean the house is gone. I can't see it anymore."

"What are you talking about? It should be right there," Yolanda said. That didn't make any sense. Where would it have gone? "We haven't gone far."

"See for yourself." Sonja jumped off Hasik's shoulders.

Ghita climbed up next. "But it can't be gone!" Her head jerked back and forth. "Where did it go?" Ghita jumped down and reached into her pocket. She pulled out her cell phone and held it over her head. "I don't have any service. What's going on?"

"My turn," Yolanda said. There was no way the house could be gone. It wouldn't simply vanish. It made no sense.

She set Rosalind Franklin on the ground and climbed onto Hasik's shoulders.

"Ouch," he said as her shoes dug into his ribs.

"Sorry!"

Way in the distance, on top of the butte, the pecan tree stood alone, covered in a dull haze. Yolanda looked in the opposite direction. All the way to the shadows of the mountain range was never-ending grass. Lush, green, vibrating grass. She squinted, hoping to be missing something quite obvious, but there was nothing. The house was gone.

Sixteen

YOLANDA hopped down from Hasik's shoulders and ran to Wela. "Where is it? Where did the house go?" It made no sense. She could see the *casita*, the pecan tree, and even the mountain range. Where had it gone?

Wela opened her sleepy eyes. "It's a strange land. There is no turning back once you enter the grass." Her head lolled back. "Take me to the tree, *mija*."

"I'm going to take you." Yolanda looked around frantically. "But they need to go home!"

"You're kidding, right?" Hasik wiped the tiny beads of sweat from his forehead with the back of his hand. "The house isn't really gone."

"What's happening?" Ghita whined.

Yolanda sat on the ground next to Wela. Rosalind Franklin climbed into her lap and licked the sweat from her cheek. This was supposed to be Yolanda's thing. By herself. Why did everything have to get ruined?

"The tree, *mija*," Wela whispered as she closed her eyes again.

Getting Wela to the tree was more important than anything else. Wela said everything would be set right when they got to the tree. Her family depended on it. As much as she didn't want them to come, this was the only way. If it meant bringing her sister and her ex–best friend along, she would just have to deal with that. Yolanda glanced at Sonja, who was frantically pushing buttons on her cell phone. A small swarm of bees ducked in and out of her braids.

And the bees. She'd have to deal with the bees.

Yolanda shuddered, remembering she'd never gotten her epinephrine refill from Mrs. Patel.

Yolanda stood and took a deep breath. She pointed at Ghita. "I don't *want* you here as much as you don't want to be here." Then she pointed at Sonja. "And I certainly don't *need* your help or interference. Or your bees, for that matter. But I'm taking Wela to the pecan tree. It's the only way to save her. And she's weak, so I can't do it by myself."

"I want to go home," Ghita whined.

Sonja shot her a look.

"That's the way to get you home," Yolanda snapped. Even with the nose ring making her look older, Ghita sure acted like a baby sometimes.

"I can't believe I came in here." Ghita shook her head.

Hasik put an arm around his sister. "It's okay. We'll get back. Everything will be okay."

Ghita shrugged him off. "Amma is going to kill us."

"No she won't," Hasik said.

"She will if we miss our flight to Kolkata in two days."

Hasik wiped the sweat off the back of his neck. "Oh yeah—that."

Sonja examined a bumblebee crawling down her arm. She looked deep in thought.

"What, Sonja?" Yolanda said. "What are you thinking about?"

Sonja squinted her eyes and bit her lip. "It shouldn't take us long to get there. Dad and I hiked there once. It's just under ten miles, and if we hike around the side of the butte, there are switchbacks—"

Sonja stopped.

"What?" Yolanda said.

Sonja glanced at Wela, who was asleep, the butterflies nestled deep in her hair. "But Wela"—Sonja ran her fingers through the blades of grass—"and this are really going to slow us down."

"That's why we brought the wheelbarrow." Hasik lifted it up.

"I think that'll help, but it's still going to be slow." Sonja cinched the backpack up on her shoulder. "We won't get there before sunset. We'll have to sleep out here at least one night."

"Sleep out here?" Ghita cried, her arms wide. "We leave in two days!"

"And that's if we don't run into any problems." Sonja swatted a bee from her forehead. It flew up and settled into her red hair.

Yolanda glanced at Wela and brushed a white curl from her forehead. "It's for Wela," Yolanda finally said. "We have to do this."

Sonja let the bumblebee crawl onto the tip of her index finger and then looked at Yolanda. "We're going." Then she looked at Ghita. "We're all going."

Seventeen

"**WE CAN** cut the grass to soften the bottom of the wheelbarrow." Hasik ripped a handful of grass from the ground and set it inside the wheelbarrow. "When she wakes up, if she's up to it, she can walk."

Sonja and Yolanda cut thick handfuls of grass with the machetes and placed them in the bottom of the wheelbarrow. Together, Hasik, Sonja, and Yolanda lifted Wela's frail, sleeping body and set her gently inside the wheelbarrow. The butterflies, disturbed, hovered above Wela for a few minutes, but nestled back in her hair as Yolanda tucked the serape in around her.

One of Wela's *chanclas* fell off, and Rosalind Franklin

snatched it and pranced around proudly. "No, no, no." Yolanda pried it from her teeth and hid it underneath the serape. "These are Wela's. She doesn't want you messing with them." Yolanda grasped both handles and lifted. "I'll push." The wheelbarrow barely moved.

"It's pretty heavy," Hasik said, reaching out to help.

"Help Sonja clear the grass." Yolanda grunted and lifted, almost tipping the wheelbarrow on its side. She heaved and righted it, determined to do it on her own.

"I'll take over when you are tired," Hasik offered.

"Just clear the grass," Yolanda said through her clenched jaw.

Hasik and Sonja each took a machete and thwacked at the grass, cutting a clear path, while Rosalind Franklin pranced her fat little body in front of the wheelbarrow, leading the way.

"Who called on the house phone?" Yolanda asked. "When we were leaving?" Surely if it was Dad, Sonja would have said something.

Sonja glanced over her shoulder. "Telemarketer."

Disappointment sank in Yolanda's gut. Still no word and it had been weeks. What if something bad had happened this time? What if this time it really was different and he didn't come back? She shook the thoughts from her mind. She needed to focus on Wela.

"Why didn't Yosemite come?" Hasik asked.

"She wouldn't." Sonja shrugged. "I called her to follow me, but she wouldn't step foot inside the grass. Rosalind Franklin, on the other hand, bolted in right after you guys."

"Of course she did." Yolanda laughed as Rosalind Franklin snorted through the tall blades of grass.

They walked so slowly it seemed like they weren't getting anywhere at all. For a while all she heard was the slicing of the machetes and the pops and clicks of the growing grass echoing all around them. From time to time Yolanda glanced at Ghita, who was last. Ghita looked back occasionally, but the path disappeared as they walked, filling up with grass.

"It's gone, Ghita," Yolanda said softly.

Ghita crossed her arms and refused to look at Yolanda, but she continued to follow the group. Even though it was hard to remember a time when they were ever best friends, Yolanda's heart ached a bit when she thought of their friendship that was . . . gone.

They'd met in Mrs. Sager's fourth-grade class, over a papier-mâché volcano. Ghita had been moved up from third grade, as third grade hadn't been challenging enough for her. The girls were paired together to paint the volcano before the big eruption.

Yolanda had been working from a realistic photograph

of a volcano in Costa Rica covered in a lush green rain-forest.

Ghita, as usual, had a different idea entirely.

"Let's paint it this hot-orange color." Ghita dipped her brush in a bright orange paint. "Like hot lava."

Yolanda's eyes widened as she dipped her brush into the soft green paint. "I think this green will look more real-istic." She did not like the idea of ruining a perfectly good volcano with bright orange paint.

"Why do the butterflies follow your grandmother?" Ghita had asked, her tongue poking from the corner of her mouth.

Yolanda swallowed hard and scooted the science book over to Ghita. "We should do brown and green—like this one." Yolanda tapped the picture with the end of her paint-brush.

Ghita glanced at the picture, shrugged, and then pro-ceeded to drop a glob of hot-orange paint on the side of the volcano.

"What are you doing?" Yolanda asked, her eyes wide.

"I think orange is better. It looks like the volcano is on fire. It'll be cool for the eruption."

"But it doesn't look anything like the picture."

"I think it'll look cool when Mrs. Sager lights it up."

Yolanda dipped her brush in the green paint again and

swirled it around the base. "I think green is better," she muttered.

"You didn't answer me," Ghita said. "Why do the butterflies follow your grandmother?"

Yolanda swallowed hard. "I don't know what you're talking about."

Ghita glanced up from the volcano, her brush in midair. "Every time she says goodbye to you at the bus stop, they are there, in her hair, the black-and-orange ones." She said it so matter-of-factly, like it wasn't strange at all, but just something she noticed.

Yolanda thought quickly. "Oh yeah, those. She and Welo—my grandfather—they study those."

"But they don't follow *him*."

"It's nothing, really. They just have them around."

"I don't believe you. I think there is something else going on. I've heard what they say. *Bruja?* What does that mean?" Ghita waved her paintbrush, splattering orange paint all over the table.

Yolanda's mouth went dry at that word. "Nothing. It's a mean word people say about us." Yolanda dipped her brush in the green paint. She needed to change the subject. "What's your grandmother like?"

Ghita sat up straight and flicked her dark hair behind her shoulder. "My grandmother—I call her Nani—is cool too. I don't mind telling you about her. She doesn't do things with butterflies. She does things with music and snakes. I want to be just like her one day."

Yolanda let Ghita talk about her snake-charming Nani and eventually gave up on trying to make the whole volcano green. They each painted a side, one green and one hot orange.

But from then on, three days a week, on the days Ghita had flute lessons, Yolanda and Sonja waited for Ghita and Hasik instead of taking the bus home. Yolanda and Ghita talked about their mutual love of books and scientific theories. They argued constantly, about all sorts of things, like whether or not time travel was possible and whether the five-second rule was real. Sonja and Hasik, always a little bored by their conversations, usually hung behind and enjoyed the outdoors, until Hasik veered off to his father's nursery to help out. But it was a few more years before Yolanda finally told Ghita the truth about Wela and the butterflies.

Eighteen

THEY walked for what felt like hours. The hot sun finally disappeared from overhead, cooling the darkening grass. Yolanda's shirt stuck to her back with sweat, and she tried to tuck her unruly curls behind her ears, but her hair was frizzy from walking in the heat and they wouldn't stay. The front wheel of the wheelbarrow squeaked with each rotation through the bumpy terrain as Wela's sleeping head lolled back and forth.

Yolanda stopped and shook out her aching arms. She didn't think she could go on pushing the wheelbarrow, but she wasn't going to ask for help. She had to do this on her own. The web of her hands burned, and when she looked closer, there were matching glistening fluid-filled blisters from the wooden handles. She lightly blew on them, soothing the pain.

"Let me take a turn." Hasik handed Yolanda the machete and pushed her gently out of the way. Yolanda reluctantly took the machete and walked in front of the wheelbarrow next to Sonja. Her hand cramped as she grasped the machete. It was a relief to not be holding all that weight anymore.

Yolanda and Sonja sliced a path ahead as Hasik, pushing the wheelbarrow, followed behind. Ghita and Rosalind Franklin were last, both of them looking tired and thirsty. But the group pressed on through the grass.

Sonja stopped. "We need to set up camp."

"Camp?" Ghita stretched her neck in an attempt to look over the grass. "We've got to almost be there. We've been walking for hours." Her cheeks were berry-red, her lips cracked.

"You need water." Sonja handed her a bottle of water from her backpack. "We haven't even made it to the *casita* yet, which is about halfway between the house and the river. Darkness will come fast, and we need to make sure we have everything set up for the night."

"We've been walking forever!" Ghita cried in anguish. She wiped the sweat from her brow with the back of her hand.

Yolanda's stomach growled. "Is the *casita* close?" She hated to stop already. This was taking much longer than she had anticipated.

"Let me see," Sonja said. She climbed onto Hasik's shoulders and looked all the way around, her hand shielding her eyes. "How strange."

"What?" Yolanda stood on her tiptoes and tried to see over the grass.

"It's as if we have hardly moved at all."

"What?" Ghita cried.

Sonja climbed down from Hasik's shoulders. "We'll never make it to the *casita* tonight. It's still too far. But we should be much closer to it than we are." Her eyes darted to Wela sleeping in the wheelbarrow.

"So we haven't moved at all?" Ghita threw her hands up. "I knew I should have never—"

"It's a strange land . . . ," Yolanda whispered, the familiar words on her lips. Did that have something to do with what was taking them so long? If it was, there wasn't anything they could do about it now. The light was fading fast. A coyote howled in the distance, sending shivers up Yolanda's spine.

"Help me cut down the grass," Yolanda said. They worked together, slicing an open area in the grass around them. The sweet scent of freshly cut grass surrounded them.

Sonja unhooked a small roll of fabric from the bottom of her backpack.

"I didn't bring a tent, so we'll have to sleep outside." Sonja unzipped her backpack.

"There should be two sleeping pads and two sleeping bags, so we can split it up. But one of us won't have anything to sleep on."

Ghita scowled.

"I don't mind sleeping on the grass." Sonja tossed a sleeping pad to Yolanda.

"Wela gets both," Yolanda said as she unrolled the sleeping pad. They placed Wela, who was still asleep, on top of the sleeping pad and zipped her in the sleeping bag, covering her with the serape. The disturbed butterflies drifted up momentarily and then nuzzled back into her hair.

Yolanda offered Hasik a pad, but he shook his head and flattened out an area of grass. Yolanda rolled a pad out next to Wela, and Rosalind Franklin wiggled between them, snorting and grunting until she buried herself between their bodies. Ghita took the last sleeping bag.

"Do we have anything to eat?" Hasik held his hand on his belly. "I hate to ask, but my stomach is aching, I'm so hungry."

"I wasn't planning on feeding so many people, so we don't have much." Yolanda dug around in her backpack and pulled out a few tamales, a piece of naan, and a banana.

"We'll have to share. Plus, we need to save something for Wela when she wakes up."

She split the items in even portions and handed them out. Had she known the others would be coming along, she would have packed much more food. Rosalind Franklin eagerly crawled into her lap and sniffed at her fingers. Yolanda shared her tamale with her, leaving her own stomach aching with hunger. The food was gone within moments, and their appetites were not satiated.

"I love sleeping outside." Sonja stretched and yawned. Ghita rolled her eyes and turned, facing away from everyone else.

The sky faded darker, from pink to blue to black, and the crickets and cicadas chirped a song through the popping grass. The stars glittered above their heads in the ink-black night as the desert air grew cooler. Hasik and Sonja were soon snoring softly, and Yolanda snuggled close to Wela to keep her warm.

She forgot how cold the desert was in the nighttime. She couldn't sleep. Yolanda quietly unzipped her backpack and dug around for the compass in the bottom. In the dim light, she held it flat. The needle spun around and around in a circle, never stopping on north.

How strange.

She checked her cell phone. It was almost eight o'clock

and her phone was almost out of battery. It wouldn't last the night, so she turned it off.

Yolanda rolled over, and the whites of Ghita's eyes shone in the moonlight as they danced around. She was awake too.

Yolanda was not going to talk to her, even if they were both awake.

It was when Welo got sick that Yolanda finally told Ghita about the family trait. It was an ordinary day, as ordinary as it could be. Yolanda and Welo were working side by side in the workshop, giving fresh milkweed to the butterflies. Sonja and Dad were off fishing, and Yolanda felt calm being with Welo. It was her favorite place to be, in his workshop, picking his brain about everything.

"We learned a little bit about genetics today," Yolanda said. "We learned brown eyes are dominant and blue eyes are recessive. And I can do this—" Yolanda stuck her tongue out and rolled it like a burrito. "And Sonja can't. She and I are so different in so many ways. It's odd we came from the same family at all."

Welo laughed. "You two certainly are different, but I think you are more alike than you realize." He handed Yolanda a thick handful of milkweed and then sat down on a stool. He took off his cowboy hat—his working hat he called it—and pushed his thick white hair back. A curl flopped over his forehead. *He looks so tired*, Yolanda had thought.

"What's wrong?" Yolanda said. "Something's wrong."

Welo glanced at Yolanda with sad eyes and gave her a half smile. "The appointment didn't go well, *mija*."

"What do you mean? What did they say?" Yolanda carefully placed a branch of milkweed inside the cage and closed the lid.

"They said—" Welo's voice caught. He cleared his throat and tried again. "They said I have a tumor, in my brain."

Yolanda's stomach dropped. "W-w-w-what does that mean?" She knew what it meant. She knew exactly what it meant. It explained everything. The headaches. The dizzy spells.

Cancer.

Cancer was Welo's biggest fear. He'd spent his life trying to avoid it. He always ate lots vitamin C and drank the newest type of green tea. If research showed something might have an effect on preventing cancer, Welo bought it and it became part of his routine. He drank green smoothies, did one hundred push-ups a day, and always put on sunscreen. It was who he was.

But all of that had been for nothing.

"They said it's aggressive, and I won't survive the year."

"A year?" The lump in Yolanda's throat caught her

breath. Or more likely less than a year. She had never con-sidered, not really considered her Welo, her *abuelo*, would ever—die. He was old, but energetic. He still had so much life left in him. What was she going to do without him?

Yolanda ran into his arms and hugged him tight, forc-ing herself to swallow the tears threatening to spill over. The pearl snaps on his plaid shirt caught on her hair, but she didn't care. This was Welo. And Welo was everything. He was the only one who got her. Who understood her. Who she understood.

Welo pulled back and looked her in the eyes. "Hey, you never know. Maybe they'll find a cure before it gets me." He pinched her quivering chin with his calloused thumb and forefinger. "They are making lots of advances every day in cancer research. Maybe something new will turn up."

But the shaking in his voice gave away that he was say-ing it only to make her feel better. And it didn't. Yolanda nodded, but she couldn't clear the lump in her throat and the dread building in her heart. He was old, sure, but why couldn't things just stay the way they were? He was every-thing to her. How would she go on without him?

After dinner that night, Yolanda rode her bike to the Patel house and banged on the front door. When Mrs. Patel opened it, Yolanda didn't even say hello or take off her shoes. She bolted through the door and up to Ghita's room. When she got there and saw her best friend, the tears finally started to trickle down her cheeks.

"What's wrong?" A look of alarm crossed Ghita's face, and she put her flute down.

"It's Welo. He's sick," Yolanda said, her voice shaking. "And I need your help. I'll do anything—anything—if you'll promise to help me. I'll even tell you about Wela and the butterflies. Just promise me you'll help me find a cure."

Ghita got up and took Yolanda's hands in hers. "Whatever you need me to do, I'll do," Ghita had said without a pause. "You're my best friend."

Nineteen

AFTER she lay there awake for a million hours, listening to the insect songs and the popping grass, the sky began to lighten, and Yolanda was ready to go. During the night, the grass had grown in all around them, enveloping them in a cool, disorienting cave. Yolanda couldn't tell which way they had come from and which direction they needed to head.

Sonja and Ghita stirred. Rosalind Franklin pushed her paws against Yolanda, and Hasik yawned loudly. Yolanda leaned over to check on Wela, who was snoring softly. Yolanda drank some water and ate half of a cold tamale. Rosalind Franklin sniffed noisily at her fingers, licking the red sauce off in desperation. Yolanda fed Rosalind Franklin the rest of the tamale and handed Hasik and Sonja each one.

Sonja split hers in half and gave it to Ghita. Ghita ate it in one bite.

"Can I have more?" she asked, her mouth full. "I'm so hungry."

"No," Yolanda said, zipping up her backpack. "We need to be careful. I have no idea how long it is going to take us to get to the tree and back. So, no more. Until lunch." She wished she had brought more food and water. They were working so hard in the heat, and who knew how long it was going to take them to get to the tree.

Hasik stood and spun in a circle with his arms out. "Which way?" The tall grass towered high over his head and surrounded them on all sides.

Yolanda climbed onto Hasik's shoulders as Rosalind Franklin barked and yelped. "Just a minute, girl. I'm check-ing—" Yolanda spotted the tree first, and Sonja was right; it looked like they hadn't made much progress getting there. She pointed. "The tree is that way. And the *casita* is over there."

"And your house?" Ghita asked.

Yolanda looked the other way. All she could see was the grass and the mountain range. The house was not there. "It's still gone." She climbed down.

Rosalind Franklin led the group, strutting ahead, while Sonja and Hasik slashed at the tall grass, making a path for the wheelbarrow. Yolanda pushed the wheelbarrow, her arms sore from all the pushing the day before. Wela snored softly, while her white curls danced over the edge of the wheelbarrow with the rhythmic cadence of the squeaking wheel.

Ghita followed, swiping a stick at the grass. "So . . . why are we taking your sick Wela to a pecan tree out in the middle of nowhere?"

"Yeah, what's the point of all of this?" Sonja glanced back. "The tree? Why are we going *there*?"

"Wela said everything will be set right when she gets to the tree," Yolanda said. "It's going to make her better."

"Is that even possible?" Sonja sliced the machete through the grass.

"That's what she said." Yolanda was not going to lose her. Not like Welo.

"And you believe her?" Hasik asked.

"Yes." Yolanda grunted and pushed the wheelbarrow over a hump on the ground. Of course she believed her. "Wela doesn't lie."

"That's true." Sonja pointed her finger matter-of-factly. "No *mentiras*."

Wela's eyelids fluttered open and she asked for water.

Yolanda unscrewed the top of hers and placed it to her lips.

"Mrs. Rodríguez, why the pecan tree?" Hasik asked. "What's so special about it?"

Wela sat up and cleared her throat. "*Mijitos*, I'm going to tell you a story."

Twenty

DURING the spring of 1943, when I was twelve years old, I lived here with my family. The land has been in my mami's family—the Rodríguezes—for many, many generations. In 1943, it was a desert, sí, but not like how it is now. My mami; my papá; my sister, Violeta; me; and my brother, Raúl, worked on the orchard, pruning the pecan trees, digging ditches for irrigation, and harvesting the nuts.

It was a successful, beautiful orchard, with rows of large, lush pecan trees that went as far as the eye could see. One night well after dark, while the lightning bugs flickered on and off, Raúl and I hid on a low branch of my favorite pecan tree.

I was practicing.

Blood sage had exploded with scarlet flowers between the orchard rows, leaving a pungent aroma hanging in the cool evening air. I had just discovered I could move butterflies and fireflies without even touching them. I had always known my skill would eventually come, but the skill with the insects was quite frankly unexpected. Raúl was amazed at what I could do.

"Josefa, how did you know?" Raúl's eyes shone in the reflection of the light from the kitchen.

"They started following me," I said. "I wasn't sure at first, but—" I danced three butterflies in a circle around his head.

He gazed at them and smiled. "Wow. I can't wait for mine to come."

"Mira," I said. "Look." I jumped down from the tree and gently touched the tiny red buds of blood sage that hadn't bloomed yet. They burst open with the touch of my fingertip.

"Wow, did you do all of this?" Raúl spread his arms wide. "The sage isn't supposed to bloom for a few more weeks."

I grinned sheepishly as I climbed back into the tree next to my brother and summoned a few fireflies into my palm.

A visitor came to the orchard that night. A visitor who would change everything. He was a man with curly black hair sticking out from a newsboy cap, rolling an enormous black trunk behind him.

Mami knew he was coming because she left out an extra plate of food for him. She'd had a dream he was coming. She was always having dreams about things that were going to happen. So while she was usually one step ahead of everyone else, it didn't mean she knew everything. She just had a feeling about things. We watched the man walk straight up the steps and knock on our front door. Later Mami told me he asked for the Rodríguez brujas and she shut the door right in his face. She hated being called that.

She said he knocked again, apologized profusely, and was actually quite charming. It wasn't every day a visitor came to our orchard, and Mami hated to be rude, so she let him in and fed him supper. After he ate, the man washed the dishes at the sink, obviously grateful for the meal. Raúl and I watched on and off through the bay window, from our place in the tree, busy with the insects.

I was letting Raúl peek inside my glowing hands when the man screamed. The fireflies flew into the night as we ran to the house, up the steps, and straight into the kitchen.

The visitor clutched his hand, blood dripping into a dark burgundy pool on the oak floor, his face pale white. Mami grabbed a dish towel and pressed it into his hand. A knife, bloodied and shiny, lay between his feet.

"It slipped while he was washing it. Get Violeta!" Mami shouted. I ran as fast as I could up the stairs to her room, but she was already coming down. She had heard the man scream too. The man began to shake, and Mami held his hand tightly, trying to stop the flow of blood. Raúl hid behind the counter, his face white.

My sister moved toward the man straightaway, pushing Mami out of the way. She removed the dish towel, and the blood oozed out of a large gash in the man's hand. White tendons were exposed in the bloody cut. She placed her hand directly on top of his hand as he winced in pain. She closed her eyes and her shoulders fell as she relaxed, taking deep breaths. The man, mesmerized, watched her every move, enchanted by the rhythm of her breath.

She removed her hand, now covered with the man's blood, and pursed her lips, blowing softly over the open gash. The dripping blood slowed. It seemed to go backward, back into the man's wounded hand, and the cut began to close.

He pushed a flop of black curly hair from his brow with his good hand as my sister met his gaze. Their eyes locked, the fire between them sending a jolt through the room.

That was the moment my sister fell in love with Benjamín.

Twenty-one

AFTER she finished speaking, Wela ate half a banana and fell asleep, weakened and too tired to continue the story. The group picked up and continued navigating their way through the tall, tall grass. Sonja and Yolanda cut the grass up in front as Hasik pushed Wela in the wheelbarrow in the back. Ghita walked with Rosalind Franklin between the wheelbarrow and the sisters.

"Was he right?" Ghita said carefully. "I know you hate that word, and I know your family has those special skills, but are you what he said?"

Yolanda reeled. "No one is a *bruja*! We are not witches!" She couldn't believe Ghita would bring that up. Ghita knew how they loathed that word whispered under the breath of passersby. How could she think that about them? "People in this town call us that because they are afraid. They've been calling Wela that since she was a child."

"Well, don't they have a reason to?" Ghita asked. "It's because of the drought, right? When she and Welo moved back, the drought came. That's what Eli told me."

Sonja rolled her eyes. "I can't believe you'd listen to anything Eli Jensen says. His mother and grandmother are the worst culprits of spreading around those rumors about our family."

"Well, did they cause the drought?" Hasik asked. "My dad said he's heard the same sort of thing. Everything died and the river dried up when they moved back into that house."

Yolanda felt the heat rise up the back of her neck. It was hard to listen to Hasik and Ghita talk about her family like that. How could they believe such things? The Patels were supposed to be their allies, the only people in town who would even speak to them. It wasn't easy to hear the way they were talking about Wela and Welo as though they weren't to be trusted.

"None of that is true," Yolanda said matter-of-factly. "You guys need to think about who you are talking to. Wela and Welo did not cause the drought."

Sonja swiped the machete at the grass. "I get how the town perceives Wela. It's not like she's made a huge effort to get to know people."

Yolanda pursed her lips. She couldn't believe Sonja was taking their side. "That still doesn't give them the right to call us *brujas*!"

Sonja looked taken aback. "I didn't say it did. I'm just saying Wela and Welo didn't help their situation any."

"Welo tried to!" Yolanda cried. "He worked his whole life to explain the trait, to figure out how to explain it so people wouldn't think it was strange!" Yolanda's heart pounded in her chest. Her own reaction surprised her. She knew she was still upset about Wela burning Welo's notes, but this was the first time it occurred to her that Welo's work was more about trying to be accepted for who they were instead of a scientific discovery. The loss felt even greater now.

"I'm not blaming Wela. She had a lot of bad things happen when she was a child. Something terrible happened to her sister. It was very tragic," Sonja said quietly.

Yolanda knew something had happened to Violeta, but she didn't know details. And it sounded like Sonja did. Why didn't Wela ever tell her anything? Why did she save all the family stories for Sonja?

"That's why it so important for me to learn how to control the bees—and pretend I'm just interested in studying them. Because when people find out about the truth, it can be dangerous."

Sonja sliced an arm through the grass, accidentally dropping the machete to the ground.

"I can help." Ghita held out a hand. "I'm sure you guys are tired."

"I don't need your help." Sonja picked up the machete and ignored her. She continued to slice the grass.

"It'll be easier if we take turns. Then everyone can have a break."

"I said no," Sonja said.

Ghita's face fell, and Yolanda suddenly felt a little sorry for her. Then Sonja's bees darted dangerously close to Yolanda.

"Here." Yolanda handed Ghita the machete. Another bee flew by her ear. "I could use a break."

Ghita pressed her lips together in an almost smile and took Yolanda's spot next to Sonja.

"Just because you said no to me at the house doesn't mean we can't still be friends," Ghita whispered to Sonja. She held the machete awkwardly and struggled to cut the grass. Sonja watched her out of the corner of her eye but didn't say anything. Ghita continued to swat at the grass without actually cutting any of it.

"Use it on an angle. It'll cut better." Sonja placed her hand over Ghita's. "Like this."

Ghita adjusted her grip and started cutting again, her eyes a little brighter, and this time with much better results. Long blades of grass flew out on either side of her.

Last summer, when Welo got sick, Ghita and Yolanda had spent all of their free time looking for a cure. Every morning before the sun came up, Yolanda waited by the dirt road for Ghita, and they walked to the college where Wela worked and searched websites, self-help books, and health magazines looking for anything new in brain tumor research that could help Welo. They even found some of the latest scientific periodicals and tried their best to understand what the articles were saying. They sat side by side, poring over articles, sharing half-cold burritos out of the vending machine until it grew dark. And every night, when she got home, Yolanda crept into Welo's room and smoothed the serape over his thinning body and whispered, "We didn't find it today, Welo, but we will. I'll keep searching. I won't give up."

Sonja would be snoring next to him, her red hair falling on her freckled face, exhausted from all of the up and down. Getting him glasses of water, bringing him meals and medicine, helping him to the bathroom. Sonja took care of him as Wela worked at the college and Yolanda desperately searched for a cure.

One evening, as they walked home, a look of concern came over Ghita's face. "Even if we do find something that could help your Welo, it won't matter. We won't be able to help him in time."

Yolanda sucked in a breath as though she'd been punched in the gut. How could Ghita be so careless with her words? Surely she didn't mean it.

But Ghita kept going. She turned to Yolanda and looked down at her hands.

"Face it, Yo—he's dying."

"How could you say something like that?" Yolanda was stunned. She blinked back tears. "That's not going to happen."

"I'm sorry, Yo. I . . ." Ghita held out her hands and shrugged helplessly.

Yolanda knew Ghita wasn't going to stop. She never did. She always barreled right through without a thought for anyone else.

"I just think you are wasting your time when you could be spending it with him."

"You promised you would help me." Yolanda glared at Ghita. "I can't believe you!" How could her best friend say such a thing? How dare she? In her heart she knew there was truth to what Ghita was saying, but she couldn't admit it. Admitting it would mean they were running out of time. Admitting it would mean that Welo was really dying. Yolanda turned, cinched her backpack over her shoulders, and ran home, leaving Ghita in the middle of the road.

The next day Yolanda didn't wait for Ghita.

And when Ghita showed up at the library later that morning, Yolanda ignored her and continued thumbing through a nutrition textbook.

"I'm sorry, Yo. I'm sorry if I hurt your feelings." Ghita picked at a hangnail. "I know this is hard for you. I'll keep searching."

But Yolanda didn't look up. Cancer would not beat Welo. Yolanda could fix this. Science could fix anything. You just had to know how to use it. And she didn't need Ghita or anyone else to help her do it.

Ghita stood there for a long while in awkward silence, but Yolanda still wouldn't utter a word.

Then Ghita pulled up a chair, sat next to Yolanda, opened her own notebook, and began to read. For the next two weeks, Ghita waited outside Yolanda's front door every morning. And they would walk in silence to the library and work side by side together.

But Yolanda still wouldn't speak to Ghita.

Ghita's words had hit something deep within Yolanda.

The fear of losing Welo and having others see it as possible was too devastating to admit. But Ghita was her best friend, and the fact that she came every day to help Yolanda changed her heart. After one particularly long day of reading, Yolanda decided she had been too harsh with Ghita. She missed her best friend and was glad that she was still helping her. She decided first thing the next morning she would apologize.

But the next morning Ghita wasn't waiting at her door. Yolanda waited until the sun came up before she realized Ghita wasn't coming at all and walked to the library alone.

Three days later Welo died.

And Yolanda never forgave Ghita. She couldn't forgive her for abandoning her right when she needed her the most.

A few weeks after Welo's funeral, Ghita came over and tried to talk to Yolanda. Wela pleaded with Yolanda to hear her out. But Yolanda refused to see her. Ghita had abandoned her, and she wasn't going to fall for that again. She watched from her bedroom as Ghita sat on the front steps, with her brand-new shiny gold nose ring, whistling away on her flute, waiting for Yolanda to come out.

Yolanda never did.

But Sonja did.

Ghita and Sonja sat on the porch, next to each other, as

Ghita played her flute and Sonja's brand-new bees swirled around their heads to the beat of the music. Ghita, her lips pressed on the flute, smiled at Sonja. Sonja's freckled cheeks shone pink.

The lump in her throat sat hard and heavy. That was the moment Yolanda realized she had lost her best friend and her sister.

Twenty-two

WELA slept most of the afternoon, waking for a sip of water and falling right back to sleep. Yolanda had hoped that after a quick stop at the *casita*, they would make it to the river by nightfall, but Sonja was right; something strange was happening. Even though the grass was dense and their progress was slow, they should have made it to the *casita* hours ago.

After the sun tipped over the highest point in the bright blue sky, they stopped for a water break. Yolanda's stomach growled as she dug around the bottom of her pack, pulling out a piece of stale naan and two brown bananas. Once they ate this, they would be out of food. Reluctantly, she split up the food and handed it out, no one daring to complain about the small portions.

Ghita stood and brushed her hands on her pants. "Hasik, I want to look for the house one more time."

"Give it up already!" Sonja threw her hands up. "The house is gone."

Ghita ignored Sonja. Hasik climbed to his feet and helped Ghita climb onto his shoulders.

"There's something over there. It's an old house." Ghita pointed. "It's not far."

"Finally!" Yolanda said, relieved. She glanced at Wela, who was still asleep. Hopefully the box she was looking for was there. "It's got to be the *casita*."

"Dad and I stopped there once," Sonja said. "Maybe we can camp there tonight."

"Camp again?" Ghita climbed down. "Amma is for sure going to kill us. We are supposed to leave for Kolkata tomorrow morning!"

"Forget about Kolkata!" Sonja yelled.

The group fell silent. No one sure what to say. Rosalind Franklin pranced around in a circle, her tags jingling. The hot sun beat over them as Yolanda's stomach growled again.

"Maybe by some miracle there will be food or water at the *casita*." Yolanda gently wiped the sweat that had gathered in the creases of Wela's face with the serape and sighed. She was looking worse. Her hair was not as bright, and her skin was more yellow than it had been.

Hasik gripped the handles of the wheelbarrow as Sonja and Yolanda walked ahead to cut the path.

"I'm worried about Wela," Yolanda said. "She doesn't look good."

"Well, of course not," Sonja snapped. "She's dying, Yo, and you brought her out here in the heat."

Sonja's attitude was getting worse by the minute. "She asked me to! Just wait. You'll see." Yolanda didn't want to talk to Sonja about Wela anymore. Sonja always thought she knew everything—about everything.

Ghita walked behind Hasik, and they could hear her huffing and puffing.

Sonja looked back and rolled her eyes.

"What's going on between you and Ghita?" Yolanda whispered to Sonja. "You're being so snippy."

"You should talk." Sonja sliced the grass in front of her. "You're the one who's been giving us both the silent treatment for half a year." Sonja picked up her pace and moved in front, her bees flying right into Yolanda's face.

"Can you get these out of my face?" Yolanda ducked down, avoiding a stray bee. "I don't have my medicine with me."

Sonja ignored her and continued cutting down the

grass in front. Yolanda had no choice but to ease back and away from the bees.

The sun pulsed overhead, radiating heat into the thick grass scratching at her legs, leaving red, itchy marks across her shins. The monotonous rhythmic squeak from the wheelbarrow blended in the noise of her thoughts.

Shortly after Sonja's bees first came, they were getting ready for bed and Sonja started pacing back and forth. She was biting her thumbnail. "I need to tell you something, Yo."

They had just returned from the hospital after Yolanda's first bee sting, and Sonja had been acting weird about the whole thing. Yolanda assumed she felt bad about the bee sting and Yolanda almost dying.

"I'm different." Sonja's voice was shaking.

"Of course you are different. We are all different in this family." Yolanda rolled the hospital bracelet around her wrist and rubbed the red spot on her arm. "One day my skill will come, and hopefully it has nothing to do with bees—or anything that can hurt anyone else."

Sonja shoulders sagged and her expression turned serious.

Yolanda faced her sister. She obviously felt really bad about the bees. It had scared all of them—Wela too. "I know you didn't mean to—with the bees. I'm okay. I really am. I'll have to learn how—"

"No." Sonja shook her head. "Not that." Her eyes darted around the room, and she pushed her red hair back from her face with both of her hands. Something was bothering her. She hadn't looked this worried since Welo got sick. "I think—"

"What?" Yolanda held her hands out. "Just say it."

"I think I like . . . girls."

Yolanda blinked. "Girls?" Then it hit her. Of course, it all made perfect sense. Dread filled her, and her gaze dropped to the floor. "You mean . . . you like Ghita?" Yolanda had noticed Sonja and Ghita spending a lot of time together.

She wasn't expecting to hear that. She thought they were just friends. Like she and Ghita had been. She thought Ghita had replaced her with a new best friend. Yolanda had assumed things would eventually go back to normal. She and Ghita would make up and be best friends again.

But now.

Now she didn't know what to think.

It was like someone had sucked the air out of the room. Sonja was her sister and Ghita was her best friend, ex–best friend. They couldn't like each other. Where would Yolanda fit in?

"Do you think Dad will care?" Sonja's voice shook.

Dad? What about me? Ghita's my best friend!

Yolanda knew her sister needed reassurance, but Ghita?

It had become too much. She felt herself falling deeper and deeper into loneliness. If she didn't have Ghita or Sonja, who did she have?

She knew she should tell Sonja is was fine, that it didn't matter if she liked girls, because that was how she really felt. She should have told her everything was going to be okay. But she couldn't bring herself to do it. Why did it have to be Ghita?

"I—I—I don't know." Yolanda shook her head. Then she got up and slammed the bedroom door behind her, leaving Sonja by herself.

As they continued walking through the grass, Yolanda's vision blurred and her legs grew shaky and tired. She glanced back at Hasik. His forehead was sweaty and his shirt soaked. They stopped for a water break, and Yolanda pulled the serape off Wela. One of her *chanclas* fell on the ground, and Rosalind Franklin scooped it up and ran ahead of the group, wagging her tail.

"Rosalind Franklin!" Yolanda scolded. She folded up the serape and placed it behind Wela's head. Wela sighed peacefully.

When they finally came to the *casita*, the sun was reaching for the horizon. There was a break in the grass in a perfect circle surrounding the *casita*. The ground was covered in hardened red earth, with green prickly pear cacti scattered around. The *casita* had obviously long been abandoned, the stone walls crumbled in places, leaving holes and gaps between the adobe bricks blackened with soot. The glass had been broken out of every window. Hasik parked Wela asleep in the wheelbarrow under a slice of shade near the porch. Rosalind Franklin sauntered proudly around the outside of the *casita*, the leather *chancla* hanging from her teeth.

Sonja stepped onto the small front porch and over a large hole in the floor. "The time Dad and I stopped here—" Sonja grasped the handle of the door and tugged. The entire door fell off its rusted screws and almost toppled her over. She let go as it clattered onto the porch, kicking up a torrent of dust and startling Rosalind Franklin, who darted behind the wheelbarrow. "Well, the door wasn't quite this bad then."

Sonja stepped inside.

Yolanda peeked through an empty window. It was a small house with two rooms. Yolanda stepped into the front room on a thick layer of red sand. Stacked against the wall near a long wooden table were a variety of rusted rakes, clippers, and shovels. A small doorway led to a back room, where waves of sand reached the ceiling and poured out of the doorway and into the front room.

Hasik stepped through the doorway carefully and

looked around. "Not much in here, just some old tools."

"Yes, but—" Sonja tugged a rusted shovel out from the sand. "This could help us dig for water." She tossed the shovel from hand to hand.

"We are looking for a box," Yolanda said as she scanned the room.

"What kind of box?" Ghita ran her fingers along the wall.

"I don't know exactly."

The sandy floor creaked under Yolanda's feet. Fading bits of sunlight shone between the gaps in the walls. Above the long wooden table, gray scratches had been dug into the adobe wall. Letters and squares adorned the length of the wall above the table. Yolanda ran her fingers into the indentions. There was something familiar about them.

Rosalind Franklin strutted into the *casita*, carrying her prized *chancla*, and looked around. Yolanda reached down to grab the shoe from Rosalind Franklin when Sonja screamed.

"Look out!"

A large speckled bobcat leapt from behind the tools and hissed at Yolanda and Rosalind Franklin, baring its pointed canine teeth.

Yolanda froze. Her heart slammed against her chest, but she couldn't move.

Rosalind Franklin dropped the *chancla* and began to growl, her black hackles rising up along her backbone. The bobcat crouched low on the ground, its eyes locked with hers. They danced around each other in a circle, the bobcat pushing Rosalind Franklin and Yolanda toward the back room and the sand-filled doorway.

Clutching the water bottle in one hand, Yolanda did the only thing she could think of. She threw the empty bottle at the bobcat, which seemed to irritate it more.

The bobcat leapt right at her. Yolanda turned and stumbled on the sand in the doorway. The bobcat's teeth sank into her shoulder, the pain searing through her entire body.

Yolanda screamed.

Rosalind Franklin sprang onto the bobcat, her teeth sinking deep into its throat. Startled, the bobcat let go of Yolanda and whipped around, flinging Rosalind Franklin off. The bobcat charged at Rosalind Franklin, and they were a tangle of limbs, sand, and fur.

No, no, no! Yolanda kicked and flailed, desperate to save Rosalind Franklin.

A spray of blood dotted the sand, and Rosalind Franklin yelped. She backed away quickly while the bobcat leapt at her again, just missing her.

Sonja threw the shovel at the bobcat and it clanged

against the wall. The bobcat backed up, leapt on the table, and disappeared through a glassless window.

Rosalind Franklin ran out of the *casita*, her tail tucked between her legs, leaving a trail of blood spots behind her.

Yolanda sat up, clutching her shoulder, shaking.

Blood oozed through her fingertips.

Twenty-three

HASIK knelt down in front of her and inspected the wound. "It doesn't look deep." He pulled an extra shirt from one of the backpacks and dabbed at it. Yolanda winced, and her hands shook. "But it could get infected," he said.

Yolanda tried to calm herself and take a deep breath, but as she looked toward the door, a surge of adrenaline coursed through her again. "Where did she go? Where's Rosalind Franklin?" Her heart pounded anxiously.

"We'll need water to wash it," Sonja said, her voice shaking. She paced back and forth across the room. "I remember a cottonwood not too far from here. I can try digging there." Sonja picked up the shovel and walked toward the opening of the *casita*. "I'll check on Wela first. I shouldn't be long."

Ghita pulled another rusted shovel out of the sand and followed Sonja.

Sonja turned back. "I don't need your help."

"You're not going alone." Ghita looked Sonja right in the eyes. "It's too dangerous."

"Take her, Sonja," Yolanda snapped. Sonja's attitude toward Ghita was starting to bother her. Hasik dabbed her shoulder again and she winced. "Can you check on Rosalind Franklin? I'm worried."

"I'm sure she just got spooked." Sonja examined the dots of blood on the sand. She poked her head out of the doorway. "Wela's okay. She's sleeping. We'll be back soon."

Hasik helped Yolanda to her feet, her legs shaking underneath her. "I need to see if Rosalind Franklin is okay," she said.

After Welo died, Dad had taken the girls to go pick out a puppy. Yolanda was immediately drawn to a fat black puppy with puffy cheeks and perky ears. She was a rowdy little thing, pulling on her mama's tail and jumping over all the other puppies. Yolanda knew what she wanted to call her.

"Rosalind Franklin," she'd said. She had learned about the chemist that week and was now officially obsessed with her.

"That name is too long," Sonja said, dragging a toy

rope across the ground for a gray-and-white puppy. "I like Yosemite or Sequoia."

Yolanda rolled her eyes. "You and your outdoorsy references."

"You and your science references." Sonja had raised her eyebrows at her sister as she picked up the gray-and-white dog. "Besides, I like this one. She's calm."

"I want this one." Yolanda picked up the black puppy and nuzzled her nose into her fur. "Rosalind Franklin." And so it was.

Rosalind Franklin.

Yolanda followed the trail of blood out of the *casita*, her stomach in knots. She scanned the area, looking for any signs of the bobcat. There were none. Wela was still sleeping peacefully in the wheelbarrow under the shade. The grass whistled as a slight breeze blew a few stray hairs across Wela's face. Yolanda swallowed hard. What if Rosalind Franklin was badly hurt? She continued to follow the drops of blood down the steps, across the red sand. The drops ended at the edge of the grass.

Yolanda parted the grass and tried to follow the drops of blood, but they quickly disappeared. She felt a hand on her wrist, pulling her back.

"You can't go after her," Hasik said gently. "You'll get lost out there."

She knew he was right. But she wanted nothing more than to go after her dog and make sure she was okay. Yolanda shut her eyes and shook her head. "I can't leave her out there all on her own." Anguish twisted inside of her as the tears brimmed in her eyes. She felt like she was abandoning her dog. She dropped to her knees. "Rosalind Franklin!" Her voice cracked. "Come back, girl!"

Hasik handed Yolanda the collar with blue and purple double helices. A small line of crimson was streaked over the *l* in *Rosalind*. Yolanda sat there for a long time, running her fingers over the embroidered letters, replaying the incident in her mind. Maybe she could have grabbed Rosalind Franklin or done something more to help her. It had all happened so fast.

"We'll find her," he said.

"Out here?" Yolanda looked at the grass surrounding them. The air chilled as the breeze whistled through the popping blades.

"She's a scrappy little thing. We'll find her." Hasik patted her on the back reassuringly.

The guilt sat like a hot stone in her stomach. She hoped they would find Rosalind Franklin and she would be okay, but Yolanda couldn't shake the dread that she might never see her again. And that Rosalind Franklin had protected her from the bobcat made Yolanda feel even worse.

Even though she didn't want to, and even though all she wanted to do was run into the grass after Rosalind Franklin and scoop her up in her arms, Yolanda double wrapped the collar around her wrist, fastened it, and climbed to her feet.

Twenty-four

"I HAVE that turmeric." Hasik pulled the bulb out from his pocket and scraped it on a rock. "It might help."

Yolanda and Hasik were sitting outside the *casita*. The sun was beginning to set, and they had moved Wela out of the wheelbarrow and onto a bed of grass. Her heart ached for Rosalind Franklin, and she wanted nothing more than to go find her and make sure she was okay, but Sonja and Ghita still had not returned and it looked as though they would have to camp another night. Her head flicked back and forth at every crunch of a twig or swish of grass. She heard coyotes howling in the distance and thought about all the horrible things that could happen to Rosalind Franklin during the night.

She rubbed the bulb over her shoulder. The juice was soothing. "I should have paid closer attention to your science fair project," Yolanda admitted. She blew cool air over the teeth marks, drying the juice and sending goose bumps down her shaking arm.

Hasik smiled, rubbing the back of his neck as he lumbered around her. "It wasn't that great of a project, just some stuff my dad showed me." He stopped. "Now, your project . . . Your project was something—something—way over my head." He laughed.

"You're really honest. I like that," Yolanda said. As soon as she said it, her palms began to tingle. She rubbed the turmeric over the marks in her shoulder a little harder.

They both looked at Wela, sleeping in the shade. The butterflies opened and closed their wings, their black-and-orange patterns glowing like a halo in her hair.

"You sure it doesn't bother you?" Hasik's brown eyes were genuine and warm.

"What?" Yolanda said.

"That you didn't get the trait?"

His question surprised her. Of course it bothered her, but she wasn't going to admit it to anyone. There wasn't anything she could do about it.

So she lied.

"Nope."

Hasik stood and stretched his arms over his head. "I still don't believe you." He shook his head. "If my sister had a skill like that and I didn't, it would definitely bother me."

Hasik was so matter-of-fact, like it was perfectly normal to feel jealous over something like that. He was easy to talk to. Yolanda sighed. "Welo told me once that Raúl, Wela's brother, never got a skill."

Hasik sat back down. "So you might end up like Raúl? Without a skill?"

Yolanda nodded sadly. "Yep."

Yolanda didn't say anything for a few minutes, the awkward silence hanging in the air. Then she finally said, "Okay, yes, fine, it bothers me."

Hasik nudged her. "But you don't need a skill. You're practically a genius anyway. That's your skill, being so smart."

Yolanda shook her head. "But I'm ordinary. Not like Wela, or my sister, or Mami, or Violeta, or Mamá, for that matter. Why do I have to be the ordinary one?"

Hasik's voice softened. "There's nothing ordinary about you."

Her fingertips prickled, her throat dried up, and she wanted to run.

"I like you," he said, and smiled.

That bright white smile.

Yolanda's insides flip-flopped and her heart began to pound again. She stood awkwardly, trying to decide if she should say something back or nothing at all. Then she dashed toward the *casita*.

"I think you might like me too," Hasik called as she disappeared inside the *casita*.

Yolanda leaned against the cool wall, her heart beating fast. The sand underneath her feet was soft and her feet sank in. *I don't like you—like that. At least, I don't think I do.* But all these feelings, the nerves, the heart pounding. Maybe she did like him.

She turned her attention to the scratches in the wall and traced the marks with her fingertips. She realized why they were so familiar.

Punnett squares.

Hundreds of them etched into the crumbling wall, with different letters and sizes, but all with the same handwriting.

The turmeric grew slippery in her sweaty hand and fell into the sand. She picked it up and dusted it off before putting it in her pocket. Something hard and black poked out of the sand underneath the table. Yolanda got down, dug in the sand, and felt something.

A handle.

She pulled hard. It didn't budge.

She peered underneath the long wooden table and pushed the sand away, revealing a rectangular metal box the size of a large shoe box. She pulled until finally it sprang from underneath the table.

Yolanda placed it on the ground next to her and tried the latch on the front, but it was locked. She shook it. It was heavy, as though it was filled with sand too. *This must be the box Wela was looking for,* she thought.

Yolanda brought it outside as Ghita and Sonja returned from their water search.

"We didn't find water." Sonja stabbed the shovel into the ground. "We dug at a cottonwood, but the ground was hard, so we didn't get very deep. The closer we get to the river, the better our chances will be to find water."

Sonja's freckled cheeks were sunburned and her lips cracked. Three bees buzzed around her head.

Ghita looked exhausted.

"Did you find her?" Yolanda asked hopefully.

Ghita shook her head, her lips pressed into a thin line.

Yolanda's heart sank and she tried to push the thoughts of an injured Rosalind Franklin from her mind. "Thanks for earlier," she said. "For, you know . . ."

"Scaring the bobcat away?" Hasik walked around the side of the *casita*, his fingers bloodied, carrying several pads of green cactus.

Sonja smiled. "No problem."

"I found prickly pear," he said. "We'll need a fire to roast the spines off, but I've heard it's pretty tasty. It's too early in the season for the prickly pear fruits. Sorry." He dropped the cactus in a pile on the ground. He paused and scratched the back of his head with his hand. "I have no idea how to make a fire."

"I'll start a fire. Since we are staying. Who knows how long it will be before we will get to eat again." Sonja walked over to Wela and brushed the hair from her face. "I can't believe it's taking us this long."

Hasik carefully pierced each pad of prickly pear on a stick and gave them to Ghita. Yolanda walked over and handed Hasik the bulb of turmeric.

"Thanks," Hasik said, their fingers lightly brushing. Yolanda felt her cheeks heat up as her eyes darted to the ground. She then turned her attention to her sister. She watched in amazement as Sonja quickly built a small fire next to Wela, like she'd done it a thousand times. Yolanda hadn't known her sister had so many skills. She knew Sonja and Dad camped and hiked a lot, but she had never been interested in what they were actually doing out there. Yolanda had always stayed back with Welo and worked with him in his workshop.

Wela began to stir. "Oh, *mijitos*, you're doing it all

wrong," she said, sitting up on her elbows. She raised an arm and called for Ghita to bring over the prickly pear. Hasik helped Wela sit up.

"Sonja, *ven aquí*," Wela said. "Come help me."

Sonja sat down next to Wela and held up one of the sticks of prickly pear.

"I'm going to show you how to bring the fruit," Wela said.

"But it's May." Hasik sat down in front of Wela. "It's too early."

"Watch, *mijo*." Wela held up her hand and touched the top of the prickly pear in three places. Tiny plum buds began to emerge from the top, quickly growing into a trio of prickly pear fruits.

Hasik's eyes widened. "How did you . . . ?"

Within seconds the juicy fruits were the sizes of limes, plump and ready to be picked.

"Now your turn." Wela handed a stick to Sonja.

Sonja bit her lip, three bees darting in and out of her braids. She touched the top of the cactus with her fingertip, but nothing happened. She tried again, but once again nothing happened. Her shoulders slumped in defeat as she looked at Wela and handed the stick back to her.

"It's okay, *mija*. Try again." Wela put the stick back in

Sonja's hand. "Deep breaths this time. Feel it out."

Sonja took a deep breath and closed her eyes. When she opened them, she touched the top of the cactus, and this time, tiny plum buds began to slowly emerge.

Sonja bit her lip, but the buds stopped growing and stayed the size of three purple peas. Sonja shook her head and handed the stick back to Wela.

"You just need more practice, *mija*. That's all." Wela touched each fruit, and it quickly swelled to the size of the others.

Before long, Wela had supplied the group with enough prickly pear fruit for dinner. Hasik and Sonja worked to cut and peel the fruit, while Ghita and Yolanda stuck the fruit onto sticks and roasted them over the fire.

"Your shoulder looks better," Sonja said, taking a bite of the fruit, the juice dribbling down her chin.

Yolanda glanced at her ripped, bloodstained shirt. The pain was gone and the bite marks nearly healed. It had been only a few hours.

"That turmeric must work." Yolanda ran her fingers along her arm. "Wow."

Wela's wrinkled face glowed in the flames. "What's that?" Her brow was furrowed. "That box. Is that it?"

"I think so." Yolanda had almost forgotten about the box. She tapped the top of it. "I found it in the *casita*, but I can't open it. It's locked. I'm sure Sonja can pop it open for us." Yolanda slid the box across the ground.

Sonja dug in her pocket and pulled out a pocketknife.

"Don't open it." Wela held out her arms to stop Sonja. "*A ver*, I want to see it."

Yolanda carried the heavy box to Wela and laid it in her lap. Wela brushed the sand off the top, and her hand shook as she ran her index fingers in the grooves. "*Dios mío*," she whispered.

"What? What is it, Wela?" Yolanda asked.

"This is it. You found it. We must take this." Wela's fingers curled around the box. Tears brimmed in her eyes, shining in the fire.

"What's in the box?" Sonja asked.

"It's time for the next part of my story," she said.

Twenty-five

AFTER my sister healed Benjamín, it was silly to think he would leave on his own. Mami knew the truth, of course. He had fallen in love with Vi. You couldn't really blame him. We'd all felt the chemistry between them. And she'd saved his hand. But no one dared tell Papá. Violeta was his firstborn. He could never admit that she was turning into a grown woman. Oh no, he would have lost his mind had he known what the rest of us knew.

Benjamín loved Violeta.

And she loved him back.

Benjamín stayed through the summer. My sister convinced Papá to let him help out on the orchard after his hand fully healed, which took a few days. He was a strong young man and a hard worker, determined to spend as much time as possible with my sister. Papá agreed because we had a lot of work to do and could use the extra help. But in the end, I think Papá might have suspected something because he insisted Benjamín stay in the adobe casita.

Benjamín moved himself into the casita the next night. I offered to help him move, as his hand was still a little sensitive and healing. And I was curious. Who was this young man who had come and fallen in love with my sister? As we walked down the center of the orchard, our path lit by an orb of fireflies, he refused to let me help with the massive black trunk on wheels. He wouldn't even let me touch it. This only made me sure I needed to find out what was in it.

During those summer nights, long after supper and long after all the lights were out, I would sneak out of the house, tiptoe as quietly as I could through front door and down the creaky steps, climb up the low-hanging branch of the pecan tree out front, and practice. The butterflies slept at night, so instead I danced fireflies in my palms and summoned them from afar. I coaxed summer buds to bloom and turned pecan flowers into nuts. I don't know why, but I enjoyed working at it alone, without anyone knowing or seeing what I was doing. And it felt good to be outside, in the warm moonlight, discovering it for myself. In private.

Some of those nights, Violeta would creep out the door and wait on the porch swing, her nightgown to her ankles, looking like an angel in all white. I would never move when she came out, for fear of her discovering me. And I knew what she was up to.

She would glance over her shoulder now and again, rocking the swing back and forth as the chain creaked, and wait.

Benjamín would arrive sometime later, walking up the center of the orchard, pushing his black curls from his brow, hands shoved in the pockets of his gray tweed pants with a wry smile on his face. Both of their faces would light up when they saw each other, as though they had been apart for so much longer than the few hours since supper. They would swing and whisper, their heads bent together. Vi would tuck her head into the crook of his arm and trace the scar across his palm with her finger.

After a little while, they would step into the orchard, holding hands. And as they walked by my tree, their blue shadows dancing between the moonlit rows of the orchard, I held my breath, terrified they would see me.

But they never did.

Night after night, I watched them. I never knew where they went or what they did. I could only guess, but they stayed out so late that many times the sun would wake me as Vi came running up the center of the orchard.

One evening after supper, while Violeta and Mami were cleaning up, Benjamín strolled back to his casita. I followed him, hiding behind the pecan trees so he wouldn't see me.

When he got to the casita, I waited until he went inside and shut the door before peering in through one of the foggy windows. He flipped the latches of the black trunk and lifted the lid. Inside was a contraption I hadn't seen before, black and shiny with different brass knobs and buttons. Benjamín lifted it carefully out of its case and set it on the table.

I wasn't a master with the insects back then, but they certainly had an affinity for me, and in the end they revealed my presence. It's hard to ignore a ring of fireflies thumping against the glass after dark. And so Benjamín waved me in without even glancing toward the window.

As I stepped into the creaky old casita, I noticed books stacked on the desk, some open to random pages, others flagged with bookmarks. Many of them had illustrations, drawings of people. But they were strange, like parts were missing or layers of skin flipped up.

"Human anatomy books," he said, fiddling with the knobs of the contraption and squinting an eye into the eyepiece on the top.

The calm in his voice gave me permission, and I stepped closer to the desk and turned the pages, entranced by things I had never seen before. "Why do they look like that?"

"They're drawings." He took one of the books into his hands and flipped to a page. "See this here?" He tapped with an index finger. "This here is the human brain. Scientists and doctors are just starting to learn about the structures of the brain and what they do. The brain controls so much of what we do, who we are, and why we are the way we are."

I sat down next to him as he flipped to another page.

"This here? These are the kidneys, the filters for the body. They are the most magnificent organ because their structures are so tiny, so minuscule, but they do all of the work, filtering toxins, returning important nutrients back to our blood, and making urine," he said.

I made a face.

Benjamín laughed. "Everyone makes urine, Josefa."

I felt my face flush. "But do we have to talk about it?" I pointed to the black contraption with the knobs. "What's that?"

"This." He stood and pushed his shoulders back proudly, a black curl falling over his forehead. He tapped the contraption with his palm. "This is a microscope."

"What does it do?" I stepped a bit closer.

"It magnifies things so you can see the tiniest of structures. Things you cannot see with the naked eye."

"Like a magnifying glass?" I said.

"Yes, but much more powerful." He opened an oak box on the desk, revealing rectangles of glass tucked in a ruby velvet lining. Crouching down, he located the one he was looking for, carefully slid it out of the box, and placed it in the microscope. While he fiddled with the knobs and squinted his eyes, I tried to read the tiny writing on the glass.

"Ah ha, here we go. Josefa, have you ever seen something so beautiful?" He guided me to the microscope. "Look right in there."

I did as I was instructed and looked into the eyepiece. At first it was blurry and hard for me to see, but after a few seconds my eyes adjusted, and the most beautiful image emerged. What at first looked like colorful bubbles turned into shining defined circles. Tiny dots marked the center of each bubble.

"What is it?" I asked.

"It's the cross section of a pecan tree branch," he said, smiling.

"It's beautiful." I peered into the microscope. "I had no idea a branch looked like this."

"It's amazing, isn't it?" Benjamín paced around the room excitedly. "Each little structure you see in there is one vital structure to how a pecan tree functions. It's absolutely astounding we can see it."

I stepped back. "What else is there?"

Benjamín pulled out another slide, a cross section of the human kidney. He explained the different structures and how they worked to clean the blood in the human body. With each slide of plants, parts of the human body, and bacteria, Benjamín grew more and more excited.

His enthusiasm was infectious and exhilarating. I had never heard of such things before. I was amazed. We stayed up late into the night, until he had explained every last slide from the box.

"How do you know all this?" I asked.

"I'm a scientist," he said.

That evening changed my life forever.

That was the night I knew I would become a scientist.

Twenty-six

THE NEXT morning, as soon as the sky began to lighten, everyone quietly packed their gear into the backpacks. No one mentioned leaving without Rosalind Franklin even though Yolanda couldn't get her out of her mind. She looked around longingly, hoping that she might saunter in from the grass. All night long she had tossed and turned, worrying about her sweet, mischievous dog.

Sonja climbed up on Hasik's shoulders and determined which direction the group would venture. They started out again, leaving the *casita* behind and heading toward the river.

"It shouldn't be taking this long." Sonja swiped at the grass with a machete.

"It's a strange land, *mija*," Wela said sleepily from the wheelbarrow.

The food from the night before had helped their hunger, but it hadn't been enough. They needed water. Yolanda tried to swallow, but her mouth was so dry, her tongue stuck to the roof of her mouth. She looked around at the popping grass and tried to take her mind off of Rosalind Franklin. Wela's story about the microscope had reminded her of the time she and Wela had looked in the microscope together.

It was a couple of weeks after Welo got sick. Wela was standing at the workbench and brushed her white curls from her face with the back of her hand. Little beads of sweat had collected in a row across the deep lines in her forehead. The butterflies nestled into her hair as she arranged her tools, a microscope, a box of glass slides, and blue dye.

"Today we are going to look at cells," Wela said. "But first, it's a bit hot and a bit dark in here." She opened the window, allowing a slight breeze inside the stuffy workshop. With a flick of her wrist, a swarm of fireflies flew in and formed a glowing ball above their heads, providing just enough light to work.

"When will mine come?" Yolanda had asked, still amazed at the skills Wela possessed.

"In time." Wela handed her a cotton swab. "Now, take this swab and scrape the inside of your cheek and then rub it on the glass slide here."

Yolanda did as she was told, and Wela prepared the slide. "What if I'm like your brother, Raúl?" Yolanda asked.

Wela shot her a look. *"Basta, mija."*

Wela set the slide into the notch in the microscope, adjusted the knobs, and peered into the eyepieces.

"Ah! Here! These are your cheek cells. Each one has a dark blue center called—"

"A nucleus," Yolanda said. "I finished the book you gave me. The nucleus of a cell contains the DNA, the building blocks of all living things. One set comes from your mother and one from your father."

Wela smiled and pushed the microscope toward Yolanda, who stood and peered into the eyepiece. "It's pretty incredible those little things are the key to life."

"Why did Welo's cells break? What went wrong?"

Wela sighed and looked at the ground. "We don't know what causes a cell to mess up its own process and replicate out of control. They are finding more and more about it, but we don't have all the answers."

"I want to save him," Yolanda said hopefully. "I want to discover something amazing to help people who are sick. Give them hope." Yolanda's heart swelled as she said it. Science had done so many things to help people's lives, and she would love to be able to add something meaningful.

Wela didn't say anything for a while, as though she was deciding what to say. "It's hard work being a scientist, but I wouldn't change anything about it. You know, *mija*"—Wela turned to Yolanda—"you've got it in you. If you are dedicated, I know you will do amazing things." After a long pause, Wela fiddled with the knobs on the microscope. "Let's see if I can stump you." She zoomed in again and refocused the lenses. "What is this?"

Yolanda peered into the eyepieces. "Oh, that's easy. Mitochondria, the powerhouse of the cell."

"Very good. But did you know the most interesting thing, or at least what I find to be the most interesting thing about mitochondria?"

Yolanda hesitated. She wasn't sure what Wela was getting at, and she didn't like to answer questions if she didn't already know the answer.

"The nucleus is not the only place in the cell where DNA lives. The mitochondria also contain DNA, but it's a special kind. Passed down from mother to child. So, those mitochondria right there contain DNA that's been passed from your *mamá* to you. From me to your *mamá* and from my *mami* to me and so on and so forth back and back until . . . well, I don't know how far, but very, very far."

Yolanda thought it over. "So, we are all connected. Daughters and sons, mothers, grandmothers, great-grandmothers."

"*Sí, niñas y niños, madres, abuelas y bisabuelas.* All of us are connected."

"Is that why we carry the Rodríguez name?" Yolanda asked.

Wela nodded. "Rodríguez is the maternal name, so while our last names can carry a hyphen when and if we decide to marry, Rodríguez is to remain with us always. I want you to remember that."

And Yolanda did. She thought of it often, that even though Mamá was long gone, they were connected—all the way back to ancestors she would never meet and names she would never know.

Hasik and Yolanda took turns pushing sleeping Wela in the wheelbarrow as Sonja and Ghita sliced a path through the grass. Wela's head lolled back and forth, her curls sticking to her forehead.

All morning they walked, the sun hot and high in the sky, the wheelbarrow wheel squeaking and the grass popping and clicking.

Then eventually and suddenly, the grass ended.

They had arrived at the edge of the river.

But it wasn't what they expected.

"How can there be no water?" Yolanda's chin dipped to her chest as her mouth went immediately dry. Her lips stuck to her teeth. "It's a river. This is supposed to be a river."

The hollowed-out pit of the river was dry and cracked, leaving a vein-like pattern etched in the earth. The lump in Yolanda's throat sat there, unmoving, threatening to turn into tears.

"I'm so thirsty." Ghita's bottom lip quivered.

Hasik pinched his eyes shut.

"We can follow the riverbed to the base of the butte and look for water along the way," Sonja said. Her lower lip had split down the center and was starting to bleed. She slid down the bank and into the deep dry bed, kicking up dust underneath her feet. Ghita followed, and then Yolanda and Hasik guided the wheelbarrow carefully down the hill and into the belly of the riverbed.

"There has to be water here somewhere." Sonja stabbed one of the shovels with a clink into the hard ground. "Ghita and I will go this way. You two take Wela and go that way."

"Look for cottonwood trees or salt cedars," Hasik called. "They grow near water."

Ghita turned back. "Let's meet back here in about fifteen minutes."

As they separated, Hasik kicked at the dirt, his dark shirt clinging to his sweaty back. Tiny black curls stuck to the wet skin on the back of his neck. He wasn't his usual chipper self.

"Thank you"—Yolanda tried to wet her lips—"for coming along."

When Hasik smiled, his teeth were extra bright through the layer of desert dust covering his face. Yolanda's throat went dry, and she couldn't tell if it was from his smile or the fact that she desperately needed some water.

"I'm glad I could help," he said.

"Me too."

They walked along the dry riverbed with no trees in sight. The side of the riverbed they had come from towered with beautiful tall green grass. The other side was dry, covered with curling cacti spines glowing in the sunlight.

"So really—there's no chance you might like me? Even a teeny bit?" He held up his index finger and thumb, making an inch with it.

Yolanda felt her cheeks flush. She checked to make sure Wela was still asleep.

"Um . . . well . . . I don't know." Yolanda rubbed the inside of her thumbs, the blisters almost healed. She wasn't sure. Did she like him? He was so kind and somehow suddenly making her nervous. He was also awfully cute, especially his bright white smile. Maybe she did like him. She looked up at his towering figure through her lashes. "I guess—maybe?"

"Maybe?" Hasik's eyes shone.

Yolanda tucked a frizzy curl behind her ear. "Maybe." That answer suited her. Not a yes. Not a no. She smiled.

Hasik let go of the wheelbarrow, hopped an extra step, and clapped his hands. "I'll take a maybe."

Yolanda looked at him out of the corner of her eye and he was smiling, and she couldn't help but smile too.

As they continued walking, they passed beneath an old bridge, the wood splintered and cracked. Hasik stood on his toes and could just reach the bottom of it. His fingers curled around a green vine and he pulled off an orange flower, twirling it between his fingers.

"Mexican flame vine." He tucked the orange flower behind his ear.

Yolanda laughed. He looked adorable with the bright orange flower against his brown skin. It was the perfect color for him.

Hasik tugged a second orange flower, sniffed it, and looped it behind Yolanda's ear. "For the 'maybe' girl," he said, their eyes meeting.

Yolanda's heart pounded against her ribs. How was he making her so nervous? She'd known him for years. This was Hasik. She needed to change the subject before she embarrassed herself.

Her gaze darted toward the ground. "How come you love plants so much?" she asked.

Hasik pushed the wheelbarrow and shrugged. "I've been helping my dad out at the nursery since I could walk, so I've been around them basically my whole life." He lowered his voice. "But really, it was this one time. He brought home a Venus flytrap and I saw it eat a fly. I've been hooked ever since."

Yolanda laughed and nodded. "That's like me. Ever since I looked into my first microscope, I couldn't unsee what I saw in there." Yolanda stretched her arms out in front of her. "It's like there's an entire world we don't even know about, under our noses, waiting to be discovered."

"It's incredible," Hasik said.

They continued bumping along the scorched riverbed, with no relief from the dry heat baking them. Yolanda wiped the sweat from her upper lip and Rosalind Franklin's tag clinked against her wrist. She shook it once more.

Hasik gave her a sad sideways smile. "She's just lost," he said. "We'll find her."

"I hope so." Yolanda didn't want to break down in front of Hasik and embarrass herself, but she felt the tears coming. "I know Wela has always appreciated your dad supply-

ing her with milkweed for her butterflies all these years."
She quickly wiped her tears away. Hasik didn't notice.

"He's happy to have the business." Hasik maneuvered
the wheelbarrow around a rock. "What about your dad?
What's he going to do when he gets back?"

Yolanda sighed and blinked the tears back. "I don't
know. He's only ever known the military life, but he promised this was his last tour." Yolanda sighed and wished
she believed him. "But I worry about him. What will he
do when he comes home? If he even makes it home. What
kind of job will he have? He's not the type to go work in
an office." There was no way Dad would be able to sit still
long enough to hold a desk job, or even put on a suit. The
only uniform he would wear was what the military told
him to wear. "He loves the outdoors, so maybe he could do
something outside."

"He'll figure it out," Hasik said.

"I hope so." But Yolanda wasn't so sure.

They continued walking along the riverbed, not finding anything that would signal water was nearby.

"I'm not seeing anything. Let's head back." Hasik turned
the wheelbarrow around, and Yolanda took over.

They bumped along the riverbed in silence until they
reached the place they'd parted from Sonja and Ghita.

No one was there.

"Sonja!" Yolanda called.

"I'm sure they're just a few minutes late." Hasik walked in the direction Sonja and Ghita had gone. He shrugged hopefully. "Maybe they found water?"

"I don't have a good feeling," Yolanda gripped the handles of wheelbarrow a little tighter. Her blisters burned again.

They walked for ten more minutes before Yolanda finally spotted Ghita and Sonja crouched on the ground. Her body went ice-cold.

"Sonja!" Yolanda set the wheelbarrow down and took off running.

When she reached Sonja, she was curled up in a ball and rocking back and forth. "It's okay. It's going to be okay." Yolanda searched her sister for any injury. It wasn't until she saw the blood smeared on Sonja's sunburned leg that she thought she might faint.

"What happened?" Yolanda said frantically. "Tell me! What happened?"

A whine escaped from Sonja's lap. Sonja uncurled herself, and there was Rosalind Franklin, with her stub of a tail wagging furiously. Rosalind Franklin leapt out of Sonja's arms and into Yolanda's.

A wave of relief washed over her, and the tears she had swallowed happily spilled over. "Rosalind Franklin! Where have you been?" Yolanda said, petting her all over her soft, dusty fur. Rosalind Franklin jumped up and licked the tears from her cheeks. "Oh, I missed you so much!" Rosalind Franklin yelped. Yolanda pulled back.

"She's hurt." Hasik pointed. On her hind leg was a deep cut, crusted with blood and dirt. Yolanda tried to look at it, but Rosalind Franklin snapped her leg back and whined.

"She wouldn't let me look at it either." Sonja climbed to her feet. "Ghita found her hobbling along. She looks thirsty—I think she needs water."

Yolanda stooped to examine Rosalind Franklin's leg. She was gentler this time, careful not to touch it. It was a deep cut, the tendons and muscle exposed. She would definitely need stitches.

"Once we find water I can clean it," Yolanda said. Hopefully they would find water soon. She placed Rosalind Franklin inside her backpack and zipped it up enough to let her head peek out from the top.

"We didn't find any water. Let's follow the riverbed south. It'll go right by the base of the butte to the trail we'll have to take to get to the pecan tree," Sonja said, the bees flying around her. "Maybe we'll spot something along the way."

And so they did. They walked down the riverbed in search of water. The heat beat down on them, radiating off the dried, cracked earth.

Yolanda's backpack wriggled. "Rosalind Franklin, what are you doing?" She wiggled harder and harder until Yolanda flicked off one strap and placed the backpack on the ground. Rosalind Franklin clawed at the zipper. Yolanda unzipped it, and Rosalind Franklin tumbled out in a puff of dust. She righted herself and then took off half hobbling, half running, the blood from her gash spraying in the dirt.

"Rosalind Franklin!" Yolanda yelled. "Come back here, girl!" Yolanda broke into a run, but within a few seconds Rosalind Franklin was out of sight. Her heart pounded. Where did she go?

When she rounded the next bend, Yolanda saw an enormous cottonwood tree on the bank of the riverbed. The gnarled roots twisted in all directions, making a space tall enough for Yolanda to walk through. A large beehive hummed high in the tree as Rosalind Franklin dug with her paws.

Then she saw it.

Yolanda smiled. They would find water here.

It was beautiful shiny brown mud.

Twenty-seven

YOLANDA and Hasik started digging a large hole in the mud, creating a pool to collect the water. Rosalind Franklin pranced around excitedly, occasionally jumping into the hole and drinking the muddy water, while Ghita and Sonja tended to Wela.

Wela stirred. "Oh, *mijitos*, you found water." Wela pressed her palm to her chest.

"What happened next, Wela?" Sonja wiped the sweat from Wela's forehead.

"What happened with Violeta and Benjamín?" Ghita asked, her eyes shining.

Wela cleared her throat and sat up. "Well, *mijitos*, in

order to tell you that part, I'll have to tell you about what I did."

When summer ended and school started again, I was busy, attempting to do as Violeta said and hide my skill from everyone. That proved impossible.

My butterflies were a beautiful plague. They especially liked to burrow in my hair during class, and with all the looks I was getting from the other students, it was all I could do to hide the truth any longer, really.

Normally during recess, I sheltered beneath the weeping willow tree behind the schoolhouse, practicing. Some days I would coax the catkins to blossom and reveal their tiny flowers. Other days I summoned the butterflies. Sometimes I sent them away. Most days I sat there and let them come to me naturally, the way they did.

One day during recess, Cynthia Purty popped her head between the curtain of branches. "Wow," she whispered.

I jumped, and the butterflies darted upward, fluttering underneath the cave of the willow tree, before settling down into a lush orange-and-black mantle on my arms. They opened and closed their wings as though they were winking at me.

Fiona, shielded behind the long branches, sucked in a sharp breath. "I knew you were a bruja."

"I'm not a bruja."

"Violeta healed my sister, Margaret. She told me so." Cynthia

stepped between the long branches of the willow tree and rested her hands on her hips. "She said when your sister came over, the pain disappeared. She didn't even have to go to the doctor to get a cast. How do you explain that?"

"I swear," I said. "We aren't brujas."

"That's exactly"—Cynthia's eyes sparkled with accusation—"what a bruja would say."

I shut my eyes and wished they would leave. "Okay, so what if I am? Who cares?"

Fiona spoke. "You know what they used to do to brujas?" She parted the branches and peeked her head inside. "They hung 'em or drowned 'em. My daddy told me."

"We. Are. Not. Brujas, Fiona." It was getting ridiculous. I don't know how many different ways I could have said it.

"Then why don't you go to church on Sundays?" Fiona stepped between the branches and shielded herself behind Cynthia.

"I don't know." I shrugged. "We just don't. We work in the pecan orchard every day. I guess . . . we don't have time for church."

"Don't have time for the Lord?" Cynthia placed her hand over her heart and fluttered her eyelashes. "Oh my, such sacrilege."

I laughed. "You sound like your mother."

Cynthia laughed, sat down next to me, and placed a finger under one of the butterflies, letting it crawl onto her index finger. "So, really, are you?"

"No," I said. "I can do special things with butterflies and other insects. Plants too. And Vi can heal. And Mami has dreams. It's a family thing."

"Can you show us?" Fiona asked, her stringy blond hair hanging in her face. She stepped closer, her hands clasped in front of her, as though she was afraid she might catch something.

I thought it over. What would be the harm? Maybe if they understood it wasn't so scary, they wouldn't be so afraid of us. Maybe they would stop using that word to try to hurt us. Maybe my family would finally be accepted in this town instead of being feared.

Then I did something I never should have.

I showed them what I could do.

Twenty-eight

"WHY do you think she showed them?" Hasik wiped his brow. He and Ghita took turns digging at the large hole in the thick mud.

"Because"—Sonja ripped one of the extra T-shirts from the backpacks in half—"she thought maybe if they actually saw, they would understand and wouldn't be so afraid."

It reminded Yolanda of Welo's lifelong mission to explain the trait. "The mystery of something is scarier than its reality," she said. She lifted her curls from her neck, letting the hot breeze cool her. It felt better not being enclosed in the tall grass. Now she could see the vast blue sky dotted with puffy white clouds. Wela was asleep again on the serape under the shade of the tree, and Yolanda stood back with her, eyeing the humming beehive hanging on a branch.

She couldn't get stung out here.

Sonja showed the group how to filter the muddy water through the T-shirt to make it cleaner to drink. Rosalind Franklin stood in the hole, her front paws in the mud, her butt up in the air. She lapped the water and then lifted her head, letting it dribble down her chin. Yolanda drank until her stomach was so bloated she couldn't drink anymore. Even though the water was slightly gritty, it was satisfying.

They lounged underneath the shade of the tree for a while, let the hole fill with water again and filled up the water bottles. Rosalind Franklin sat happily in Yolanda's lap as she pet her back over and over again. She squeezed her tight and nuzzled her nose into the dog's fur, breathing her in, relieved she had returned. And was safe.

Yolanda picked up one of the water bottles and squirted water on Rosalind Franklin's hind leg. The dog flinched, but Yolanda gripped her tight and washed the wound. The bloody water poured from the gash, ran down Rosalind Franklin's leg and into the dirt. Yolanda stretched her hind leg out with one hand and took a deep breath in. Then she blew the dog's fur over to one side to get a better look at it. White tendon and fatty tissue was exposed.

She definitely needed stitches.

"Hasik, do you still have that turmeric?" Yolanda asked. Hasik pulled the orange bulb from his pocket and tossed it to her. Yolanda scraped it on a rock, exposing the juicy orange root, and rubbed it over the gash. Rosalind Franklin whined.

"I don't think that will do much," Ghita said. "You should have it looked at."

Yolanda rolled her eyes. "Thanks. I'll get right on that."

"You know what I mean—when we get back."

Yolanda ripped a corner of the T-shirt they had used to filter the water and wrapped Rosalind Franklin's leg, tying it in a tight knot.

Rosalind Franklin hopped off her lap and hobbled away, shaking her leg, trying to get the bandage off. She bit at it a few times and then shook it one last time before surrendering, walking in a circle, and lying down with her chin on top of her crossed paws.

Wela woke and Yolanda helped her sit up and drink water. She had aged on their journey. Her hair was not as curly and had changed to a dull gray from the bright white it normally was. Three butterflies left her hair, perched on the wet ground, and drank. Wela didn't speak, her fingers pressed around the box in her lap, her gaze distant and vacant.

What was in the box, and why was Wela rattled so badly when she saw it?

Yolanda sat back on her heels. She followed Wela's sad gaze to the pecan tree. Only the top was visible from the riverbed, its branches twisted and black. Yolanda didn't want to think about the mountain they were going to have to climb to get there. But one thing was certain.

They were getting closer.

"Wela? What happened to Benjamín and Violeta?" Ghita asked.

"Well, *mijitos* . . ."

Twenty-nine

AFTER Benjamín showed me the microscope, we became friends. When he wasn't with Violeta, he worked hard on the orchard and asked me a thousand questions. "What does it feel like? How do you control it? When did you find out you could do that?" He asked me to show him. I danced butterflies and fireflies around his head and coaxed flowers to bloom as we walked in the orchard. I showed him. Proudly.

But after some time, it felt like my skills were all he was interested in. His questions grew incessant, and I began to wonder about him. "What are you doing here? Why are you here working on a pecan orchard if you are a scientist?" His answers never satisfied me.

One night, after Benjamín and Violeta strolled back toward the house, I snuck through the orchard all the way to the casita. I don't know what I was looking for really. Just anything that could explain what he was doing here. I looked through his slides and rifled through his books.

Hidden in the false bottom of the black trunk, I found dozens of journals filled with his notes. There were hundreds of names. Countless years and locations all over the country. Tales of special abilities, witchcraft, and unbelievable talents.

There was a list of names. Women who had been accused of practicing witchcraft. Their fates were next to their names. Drowned. Hung. Just as Fiona had described. My stomach soured as I touched each name. All those women, murdered. They could have been us. Why did Benjamín have all these names? What was he studying?

Near the bottom, I found an entry in a journal with our name.

Rodríguez
The Rodríguez brujas of McClintock, New Mexico, have owned a pecan orchard for numerous generations. Rumors in town say they are a family with a long maternal line of brujería and special abilities.
 The mother, "Mami," appears to be a clairvoyant of some sort. Although she denies ever hearing of the

brujas when asked about it, she had an extra place set for dinner on the night I arrived, leading me to believe she knew I was coming.

Oldest daughter, "Violeta," is a curandera or healer. The rumors of her abilities are the most discussed in town and the most interesting to me.

Conversation on May 12, 1943, with (16 y.o.) Margaret Purty: "A few years ago, when I was playing during recess at school, I fell from a tree and broke my arm. The bone was sticking out, and dizzy from the pain, I couldn't breathe. Violeta Rodríquez immediately ran over, crouched down, and grabbed my arm. I screamed from the pain. She told me to close my eyes and take deep breaths, so I did. I felt cool air on my arm, and then the pain was immediately gone. When I opened my eyes, the bone wasn't sticking out anymore and there was a dark pink mark and a small bit of dried blood. See here—that's the scar." Margaret Purty has a two-inch thin silver scar on the outer portion of her left forearm. She denies ever seeing a doctor for this injury.

The second daughter, "Josefa," has an ability to work with nature. She can control insects—butterflies in particular—and she can also induce flowers to bloom. I've witnessed her turn pecan flowers into nuts as well. She is smart and curious and is still learning to harness her abilities. It is quite beautiful the way she works with the butterflies, like waves in the ocean.

The youngest, a son, "Raúl," is ten, but no skill has presented itself for him yet. The skill seems to appear around the age of eleven or twelve, with slight variation. The father of the family does not have any sort of special skill or carry the Rodríquez name. This trait appears to come from the maternal side of the family.

I flipped the page over and read his account of how he cut his hand on purpose to see if Violeta could heal him. His words were clinical and matter-of-fact, leaving me to wonder if he really loved my sister after all.

I was sick to my stomach. Benjamín was here to study us and perhaps expose us. What if what happened to those other women happened to us? I had to fix this.

I took the journal back to our house and waited until morning. Then I showed Papá.

By lunchtime, Benjamín, his black trunk, and his slides were gone. Violeta refused to leave her room for weeks, completely heartbroken. I knocked on her door and tried to explain.

"Vi, he was going to expose us—you didn't read what I read. They murdered people like us."

I'll never forget the look she gave me from behind swollen, red-rimmed eyes before she shut the door in my face.

I had betrayed her. Nothing would make her trust me again.

Her love was gone, and it was all my fault.

Thirty

WELA fell asleep after the story, and they decided to rest a little longer by the riverbed to stay close to water. Sonja and Ghita built a small fire at the base of the cottonwood tree, and Hasik went to collect pads of prickly pear cactus to roast.

"Do you think that was what Benjamín was really there for?" Ghita prodded the fire with a stick. "To expose them?"

"I don't know," Sonja said, twirling a burnt stick in the air and letting the smoke curl around them. "It seems like he really loved Violeta."

"But he wouldn't have turned on them." Yolanda had never understood why everything about the trait had to be kept a secret, but now, with the mention of murders, her stomach tightened. She was beginning to understand.

After Hasik returned, they roasted the pads of prickly pear in the fire.

"Did you know I was the bigger twin?" Sonja said to Ghita as she thrust a pad of cactus into the crackling fire.

"You were only bigger because you stole all *my* resources." Yolanda rolled her eyes. Sonja always bragged about being the bigger twin when they were born, like it was some sort of advantage she had had since birth.

Yolanda pet Rosalind Franklin, who was dozing in her lap. The T-shirt bandage was dirty and beginning to fall off. Yolanda tugged at it and looked at the wound underneath. Oddly enough, it looked as though it was beginning to close. The white tendons and fatty tissue were covered with fresh pink skin. Yolanda gently rubbed it with her thumb.

"Wela told me the story of our birth." Sonja's eyes twinkled. "Do you want to hear it?"

A twinge of jealousy knotted in Yolanda's gut. Why was Wela always telling Sonja important things and telling her nothing? It wasn't fair. Yolanda did want to know. She had always wanted to hear about Mamá and the day they were born, but no one would talk about it. "It's too painful, *mija*," Wela would say as a gloomy look came over her face. Dad and Welo were no better, and eventually Yolanda stopped asking.

"Yes." Yolanda sat up straight. "Tell me."

Sonja stepped around the fire and sat cross-legged next to Yolanda. "Wela said from the start Mamá knew something was wrong. It was as if she knew all along she wasn't going to make it. She would tell her things like 'Take care of my girls and always make sure they know how much I love them.'

"Toward the end of her pregnancy, a few days before we came, Mamá began to swell. Her feet, her hands, her face. She felt terrible. She could hardly walk. She was dizzy and tired and saw flashes of light in her eyes. When Dad came home and took her blood pressure, it was dangerously high, so they raced to the hospital. When they arrived, Mamá could barely see. The flashes of light and halos in her vision blinded her."

Wela woke, her eyes glistening with tears. "Oh, *mijas*, the day you were born was the happiest and saddest day of my life all at once." Tears spilled over her cheeks as she sucked in a sharp breath and pressed a palm to her chest. "Let me finish the story.

"The doctor told us she was very sick and she needed to deliver right away. There was no time for an epidural. They needed to put her to sleep. But your mamá refused.

"'No. My babies need me,'" she said. She was calm but firm.

"'But, Alejandra, your life is in danger. You could die.'"

"She stood her ground.

"And so they prepped her for surgery, placed the needle in her back, and began to cut her as soon as she was numb. By then her blood pressure was so high, she couldn't see at all—her vision was completely gone.

"Sonja came first. When I saw her, I was scared she was bleeding from the head, but then I realized she had your father's red hair." Wela turned to Sonja. "You turned pink and screamed immediately, and we all breathed a sigh of relief. When they put you next to your mamá, even though she could no longer see you, she breathed you in, kissed you, and you calmed instantly."

Wela turned to Yolanda. "Then you came. The smallest human I have ever seen. You were covered with black hair all over your body. And you were blue. The nurses and doctors tried everything to revive you, but they said you were too small. Born too soon for your size. But your mamá, from underneath the blue layers of fabric, said, 'Bring her here.' And your father picked you up in his big arms, your tiny body flopping gently in his hands, and brought you to her. He laid you against her warm cheek. She smelled you and kissed you. Then, with her last breath, she blew the healing breath over you.

"Your tiny blue body began to pink up, and your fingers curled. Then your toes. And then the most glorious sound I have ever heard. Your cry."

Tears dripped down Wela's cheeks, and she wiped them away with her palm.

Yolanda stood, walked around the fire, and sat beside Wela. "Why haven't you ever told me that story before?" She put an arm around Wela. Her throat was tight. She'd always known Mamá hadn't made it. It had framed her entire life. It was why she lived with her dad and *abuelos*. But to hear the truth from Wela was devastating. She imagined her dad and *abuelos* standing there holding two infants and losing their wife and daughter at the same time.

"It was so hard, *mija*. I lost a piece of my soul that day— even though I gained you girls."

Yolanda cleared her throat. "Why did you tell this to Sonja?"

"I knew eventually I would tell you both. But I told her first because her gift came first, and I needed her to understand the power she held inside her. That we all hold inside of us."

A realization washed over Yolanda. Mamá had saved her life. She had sacrificed herself so Yolanda could live. "So, Mamá—she could heal . . . like your sister? Like Violeta?"

Wela nodded, the flames from the fire dancing in her eyes. "Your Mamá's gift was healing, like my sister, Vi."

After Wela finished her story, everyone but Yolanda dozed under the cottonwood tree for an afternoon snooze. She couldn't stop running the new information through her mind.

It all made perfect sense. Mamá was a medic in the army and had saved Dad's life. She must have healed him, too. Yolanda's heart was fuller after that, knowing what Mamá had done for her, someone she resembled so much but knew so little about. But something still wasn't sitting well with her.

Mamá sacrificed herself to save Yolanda. She refused to let the doctor put her under anesthesia because she knew she would have to be awake to save her baby.

To save Yolanda.

Then she thought about Dad and how devastated he must have been about Mamá's sacrifice and to be left alone with two baby girls.

The ability to heal was wonderful, but also quite frightening.

The thought gripped her. Maybe it wasn't such a bad thing she didn't have a gift.

Wela had called it a beautiful plague.

Maybe it was a plague.

Thirty-one

YOLANDA woke to the sun piercing through the cotton-wood branches. She must have fallen asleep after all. She yawned and stretched. She was getting better at sleeping outside. When she rolled over, she saw Wela was awake, playing with the latch on the metal box.

Yolanda tucked her arm under her head. "I hope telling us the story didn't make you too sad."

"That story always makes me sad, *mija*." Wela brushed the dust off the top of the box. "But it's no one's fault. It's just how it is."

One by one the others woke and rolled over. Sonja yawned, and Hasik stretched his arms above his head.

Ghita rubbed her eyes and sat up. "So, what happened to Violeta?"

A few months later, a letter came from Benjamín. I saw it before anyone else, snuck up to Vi's bedroom, and placed it on her pillow. I thought maybe she would forgive me if I got the letter to her before anyone else saw it, but what she did was so much worse than I could have imagined.

When Violeta went up to her bedroom later that day, I followed her and watched through a crack in the door. Her eyes darted nervously around, making sure she was alone. She ripped open the letter and read it. As her fingers brushed her lips, she pressed the letter to her chest and closed her eyes. From under the bed, she pulled out a small suitcase and tucked the letter into the cream lining. In went her best pair of brown shoes, two dresses, and undergarments. She latched it shut and swept it under the bed with the heel of her foot. A smile escaped from behind the fingertips pressed to her lips. Before she could see me, I crept back to my room. I waited until my sister went down to the barn before I ran back upstairs and read the letter.

Mi amor Violeta,
My draft number came up and I must go. But I will not go to war. I will flee the despicable nature of war. I cannot take part in the death and destruction of human life. It is much too precious to me. I bought you a

bus ticket and I hope you will come to me. Run away with me, mi amor. Meet me on September 22 on the midnight train to Dallas. We can marry and hide in Mexico or anywhere else you want to so we can be together forever. I am desperate for you.

Te amo,
Benjamín

My heart sank. She had already packed her bags—it wasn't even a question to her whether or not she would go. She didn't care about the truth. She was going to leave our family and be with him.

With Benjamín.

It would devastate our family if she left. I didn't want to betray her again, so I did what I thought was best. I confronted her about the letter and made sure she understood the truth.

"He will tell everyone about us!" I said. "They killed people like us! Don't you care?"

Violeta paced back and forth across the porch. It was late, and everyone else in the family was already in bed. "But I love him, Jo. I love him." She wrung her hands. "I don't believe he came here to hurt us. That's not who he is. We fell in love. It doesn't matter to me what his intentions were when he came here. It matters what they are now. I want to be with him."

She wasn't listening to me. I couldn't change her mind.

I had to make sure she wouldn't meet him. So I asked Cynthia for her help. Before dawn, on September twenty-second, I snuck into Violeta's room and took the bus ticket while she slept.

Later that afternoon Violeta screamed as she fumbled through her suitcase. "Where is it, Jo?"

"You can't go." I said. "You can't leave us." I chewed the inside of my lip and held the bus ticket in my hands, folded like a paper bird. "I'm sorry, Vi. I can't let you do this."

Three butterflies flew underneath the folded paper and I let go. Their wings gently flapping, they carried it through the open window and down to the center of the orchard.

"No!" Violeta ran to the window.

"I'm sorry," I said. "I'm so sorry, Vi."

Thirty-two

WELA, exhausted again, was back to sleep before Hasik and Yolanda had lifted her into the wheelbarrow and covered her with the serape.

As they were about to leave, Hasik said, "Uh-oh."

Yolanda closed her eyes. This didn't sound good. "What?" she said. She followed his gaze to the wheelbarrow.

The tire was flat.

Hasik attempted to push it, but it didn't budge.

Wela's butterflies perched in her flat gray hair as she snored softly.

They were stuck.

"What are we going to do?" Hasik dropped the handles

of the wheelbarrow. "I can try to carry her, but I don't think I can do that for long."

Yolanda clenched her fists and looked up at the mountain they would have to climb. Even in the wheelbarrow, the task had seemed close to impossible. But now, with a flat tire, how would they ever get Wela up to the tree?

Sonja sat on a nearby a rock, moving a group of three bees into concentric circles between her palms as Rosalind Franklin nipped at them. As much as Yolanda didn't want to admit it, only Sonja could solve this problem.

Yolanda walked over to Sonja, with each step hoping that she could come up with a solution, a different one, where she didn't need Sonja or her skill, but she knew in her heart this was the only way. She needed her sister.

"How much control do you have?" Yolanda tucked a frizz of curly brown hair behind her ear and ducked as a stray bee whizzed by her head. "Of the bees?"

Sonja looked up, and the bumblebees buzzed faster and faster, as though she were juggling them. It was amazing how they flew and didn't collide.

Yolanda shifted back, away from the bees.

"Why?" Sonja asked.

Yolanda paused, not wanting to say the words, not wanting to need Sonja's help, but Wela's story had given her an idea. "I'm wondering if we can use your skill," Yolanda said, "to, you know . . . move her."

A puzzled look crossed Sonja's face. "How would that even work?"

"Well, all right—if you don't think . . ."

"Wait." Ghita jumped up and walked over. "What are you thinking?"

Yolanda peeled the serape from Wela and laid it on the ground. "This might sound crazy, but if we can get the bees to work together, maybe they can make this blanket . . . fly." Yolanda smoothed the fabric of the serape with her palms. "Like Wela's story with the bus ticket. She got the butterflies to carry it." Yolanda pointed overhead. "There's a beehive in the cottonwood tree. An entire swarm of them."

"I don't know . . ." Sonja chewed the inside of her cracked lip and ran a hand along her braid. "I don't know if I'll be able to. And even if I could, I don't think it would hold her."

"You could at least try," Ghita said. "What else are we going to do?"

Sonja didn't seem convinced, but Ghita was already halfway up the tree, so Sonja followed with a machete. Hasik and Yolanda straightened out the serape while Rosalind Franklin tugged at the *chancla* precariously hanging from Wela's foot.

"Do you think this will work?" Hasik knelt and flicked a speck of dirt off the serape.

"I have no idea, but it's our only hope to get moving again." She glanced at Wela, who was looking more frail with her dulling gray hair and sunken eyes. "We are running out of time."

When Sonja returned, bees surrounded her as she held a papery gray nest in her hands. Yolanda instinctively stepped back as Sonja approached and set it on the ground in front of the blanket.

Ghita grabbed the fringe on one side of the blanket while Hasik took the other, spreading the serape between them and holding it taut. Rosalind Franklin lay under the shade of the wheelbarrow, the brown *chancla* between her paws, and gnawed at the leather.

Yolanda watched as Sonja concentrated on the nest and the bees began to emerge. A couple at first, one at time, joining a swirling ball of bees in between her palms. The ball grew larger and larger and the buzzing louder and louder as Sonja spread her palms apart until the swarm was the size of a basketball. Ghita and Hasik held the blanket up over their heads as Sonja slowly walked underneath the blanket with the buzzing ball. When she flattened her palms, the swarm spread out and formed a blanket of its own, made up of buzzing bumblebees. Sonja walked out from underneath the blanket, leaving the bees behind.

"Now—slowly lower the blanket onto the bees," Sonja instructed.

Ghita and Hasik lowered the blanket on top of the bumblebees. One edge of the blanket fell, and Sonja spread out her hands, moving bees to that corner. The blanket evened out, floating above the ground.

"It's working," Sonja said, a slight surprise in her voice.

"It sure is," Yolanda said. Relief washed over her. Now if it would only hold.

Sonja pushed her hand down in the center of the blanket to test the weight, but it crashed down into a colorful heap. Bees angrily flew out from underneath the blanket. Yolanda bolted as fast as she could away from the swarm. As Sonja worked to calm them, Wela stirred from the commotion.

"Where are we?" she asked sleepily.

"We have a flat tire, and we can't move the wheelbarrow. We need your help," Yolanda said. "I thought we could move you on the blanket. Sonja got the bees to fly underneath it and hold it up, but it won't hold your weight."

Sonja held the swarm of buzzing bees between her palms again.

"I can help with that." Wela sat up, stretched her arms, and closed her eyes.

They waited for what felt like forever before the butterflies arrived. They trickled in slowly, first the white ones, then the black-and-orange monarchs. And finally, the blue butterflies. They landed on Wela's outstretched arms. Their wings opened and closed, and before long her arms were covered in them.

Ghita and Hasik straightened the serape once more. Sonja flattened the ball of bees underneath it as she had before. Ghita and Hasik gently laid the blanket on top. Yolanda helped Wela climb to her feet, careful not to disturb the butterflies on her arms. Yolanda snatched the *chancla* from Rosalind Franklin and slipped it on Wela's foot. Wela walked, slowly, toward the blanket, her white gown skimming the dusty brown earth. Her eyes were closed.

When she opened her eyes, the butterflies left her arms, flying straight up before swooping underneath the blanket and disappearing. Wela stepped toward the blanket.

"Are you sure?" Yolanda asked.

"I trust them, *mija*."

Ghita and Sonja helped Wela climb onto the blanket. The blanket sank down slightly in the center from her weight, but it held her. Sonja set the papery beehive near her feet.

Yolanda breathed a sigh of relief as Sonja and Ghita pulled Wela down the center of the riverbed. It had worked.

The blanket floated along the riverbed as though the water was actually flowing.

Yolanda kept her distance, and Hasik and Rosalind Franklin hung back to keep her company. It was nice to not have to worry about walking through the grass anymore, even though the dry desert heat radiated off the riverbed. Everyone seemed to be in much better spirits now that they had water in their bellies.

A little while later, Sonja peeled away the papery outside of the nest and broke off bits of honeycomb, handing them out. The sticky, sweet honey dripped down Yolanda's chin, and she ran her thumb along it and scooped it into her mouth.

"What happened to Violeta?" Sonja bit into a piece of honeycomb. "Something bad happened to her, didn't it? Was it Benjamín's fault?"

Wela looked sadly down at her lap. "No, *mija.* It was my fault."

Thirty-three

I TOLD Cynthia not to do anything dangerous. I told her it was just to scare my sister. She asked if Fiona could help, and while I didn't think it was a good idea at first, I agreed.

I thought she was my friend.

But she wasn't. She was just like the rest of the town.

She didn't listen.

After the butterflies flew away with the bus ticket, I knew Violeta would follow them, and I knew exactly where they were going. I watched from the window as Violeta ran down to the center of the orchard.

"Something's not right," Mami said from the doorway. I glanced up. Her fingertips were pressed against her forehead, one *of my dresses in her hand.* "Something's not right."

I took the dress from her and placed it on my bed. "It'll be okay, Mami. I'm taking care of it."

A terrified look crossed her face. "Something's not right."

I pushed past Mami, down the steps, and ran as fast as I could, staying behind Violeta, making sure she didn't see me. I hid in the pungent blood sage until she crossed the bridge over the roaring river before I made my way across. When she reached the foot of the butte, the butterflies danced around a large circle of white rocks on the ground. Large dried tumbleweeds had been piled in the center, as tall as Violeta.

The butterflies dropped the bus ticket inside the circle.

Violeta set her suitcase down, stepped inside the circle, picked up the bus ticket, and smiled.

Then, from behind the trees, the girls stepped out. Cynthia wasn't alone. Her sister, Margaret; Fiona; and four other girls from our school were all there, carrying torches of fire.

I ducked behind a tree. What were they all doing here? It was only supposed to be Cynthia and Fiona.

Violeta's eyes widened as the girls approached her, the torches lighting her face.

"Violeta Rodríguez, we hereby declare you a bruja," one of the girls said.

Fiona's stringy blond hair covered her eyes. "Brujas are made by the devil and must be . . . extinguished."

Violeta backed away.

She tripped and fell into the pile of tumbleweeds.

The group of girls stepped forward and surrounded my sister, trapping her in the center of the circle.

My heart pounded. I had to do something. I'd read Benjamin's notes. I could guess what came next. I revealed myself from behind the tree. "We aren't what you say!"

Fiona turned and glared at me, the fire from the torch lighting her sunken eyes. "You are," Fiona said. "You showed us what you can do. Brujas must be burned."

The girls closed in on my sister, the circle around her getting smaller and smaller. Violeta's eyes flashed in the fire. Her fingers curled around the bus ticket.

I didn't know what to do. I didn't know how to stop them.

So I did what I knew how to do.

I summoned them.

I summoned everything that would come. The butterflies, bees, fireflies, moths.

I wasn't sure I could do it. I had never tried before.

But they came.

It started with a low hum, and it took longer than I thought it would. But as the cloud of insects descended upon them, the girls flailed and screamed. Their torches flew all over. Cynthia screamed, dropped her torch, and ran back toward the house. The flames crackled and popped in the dry tumbleweeds, lighting the nearby underbrush.

"Josefa!" Violeta cried. "Run!"

I pressed the swarm of insects at the girls, driving them one by one away from my sister. The girls ran toward the house. But a line of fire had grown up between me and my sister, keeping us from each other.

"Vi! Come on!" I yelled. "Run through the flames. You can heal yourself afterward."

Violeta shook her head and picked up her suitcase and bus ticket. "I'm going to Benjamín."

"No, Vi! You can't!" I cried, reaching for her. The flames licked higher and higher, catching the lower limbs of a pecan tree, the smoke burning my eyes.

She coughed. "If I just get over the butte, I'll be there in no time. I'm sorry, but now you see what this town thinks of us. I can't stay here."

She blew me a kiss. "Te amo, Jo."

Then she turned and started up the trail. It was the last time I ever saw her.

Thirty-four

WELA had fallen asleep again, hovering on the humming bees and butterflies, while Ghita and Sonja pulled her along up ahead, the heat radiating off the dry earth. Yolanda was thinking about Wela's story and the girls with the torches. No wonder Wela had always been so secretive about the skill. It must have been frightening to have them attack her sister that way. Yolanda's gaze wandered up the butte. The pecan tree wasn't visible from where they were, but they were definitely making progress now.

"She looks peaceful," said Hasik.

Wela's hair was limp, the curls flattening and losing

their bounce. Her fingers were slack around the metal box on her lap.

"She does look peaceful. But she looks very weak too."

"I lost my Nani—my grandmother—last fall. Around the same time you lost Welo," Hasik said. His feet scraped against the earth. "It was hard."

"Didn't you visit her most summers?" For years, Ghita went to India for a few weeks each summer, while Yolanda counted down the days until her return.

"We did." Hasik nodded. "My mother took us to her last show. We didn't know it was going to be her last show though. She was a snake charmer—you know, she had a knack with the music. She could get the snakes to move in ways I had never seen before."

"Snake charmers aren't real." Yolanda raised her eyebrows. "I read about it once. The performers usually defang the snakes to keep them from biting."

"I'd heard that too," Hasik said. "But Nani was a real snake charmer. I've seen it. She tried to teach me how to play the punji, but I never could get the hang of it. Ghita is pretty good at it."

Yolanda thought of Ghita and Sonja's science project. The honey, the music, the bees. "Is that the little flute Ghita carries around?"

Hasik wrung his hands. "It was Nani's. My mother took

us for a visit, and she died while we were there. The men in the family are supposed to perform the funeral rites, but Nani had two daughters—my mother and my aunt. My mother asked me to help, but I . . . couldn't. I was too afraid. It was the first time anyone I knew had . . . died."

They walked a few more minutes, neither one saying anything at all. Yolanda thought back to when Welo died and how Wela asked her if she wanted to see him one last time.

To tell him goodbye.

Yolanda had fled into the desert. She couldn't see him like that.

She pinched her eyes shut and swallowed back her grief.

"But Ghita did," Hasik continued. "Ghita helped wash Nani's body. I feel so bad—I watched from the hillside as my mother, my aunt, and Ghita bathed her and wrapped her in an all-white cloth. They took such care with her. Then they laid her body on a row of wooden slats by the river." Hasik cleared his throat and looked up to vast blue sky. His eyes were wet. "I knew what was coming next, but I still wasn't ready for it." He stopped and looked at the ground. "They set it on fire."

Yolanda sucked in a breath. "Why did they set her on fire?"

"In our culture burning the dead ensures the person is released from their physical body so they can be reborn." Hasik scratched his head. "At first it was scary. I'd seen it in movies before, but it was the first time I'd ever experienced it in real life. And it was Nani, which made it even harder. Now I guess it's okay. It's what we do. What else would they do?"

"I guess it's not different from what happened to Welo." Yolanda thought of Welo's urn on the bookshelf. "Death is scary—I don't think I could do what Ghita did."

The two of them walked along in silence again. Ghita and Sonja were talking ahead, pulling Wela along as Rosalind Franklin sniffed at the dirt.

Hearing Hasik talk about his grandmother made her sad, because it made her think about Welo and losing him all over again. But it also made her feel better in some small way. Hearing him talk about his feelings about death made her feel less scared about her own feelings. "I refused to believe Welo would die. I really thought I could save him—I couldn't. I didn't."

"No one can beat death," Hasik said.

His words stung. Yolanda thought of Wela and the pecan tree and hoped Hasik was wrong. Maybe Wela was different. She had the tree. Wela's words, "it's a strange land," rang in her ears, and Yolanda felt calm. Once they got to the tree, everything would be set right. She knew it in her heart.

Rosalind Franklin chased a blue-tailed lizard to the edge of the riverbed, but came back quickly, refusing to leave the group again. Ghita turned, and the golden ring in her nose glinted in the sunlight.

"Is that when Ghita got her nose pierced?" Yolanda asked. The timing would have been right around then.

Hasik nodded. "Nani wanted her to get it when she turned twelve, like she and my mother did, but Ghita had refused, worried about what everyone back here would think. Right after the funeral, Ghita did it. She wanted to. For Nani."

Yolanda felt the shame warm her body. She had thought Ghita was trying to be cool with her nose ring. She couldn't believe her best friend had gone through so much last fall and she never knew about it. They were supposed to be best friends. Yolanda had been so selfish and focused on Welo, she never even thought about Ghita. "Wait, when did this happen?"

"We left a few days before Welo died and came back a few weeks later. I know Ghita felt terrible she wasn't here for you."

That must have been why Ghita suddenly disappeared. If only Yolanda had talked to her, maybe she would have known the truth. Yolanda felt sick to her stomach when she thought about it. She'd been so wrapped up in herself. Poor Ghita.

As they reached a widening in the riverbed, a carpet of pink flower buds covered the dry, cracked earth. "Wow." Hasik bent down and plucked a blossom. "A wildflower bloom."

Rosalind Franklin sniffed at one of the blossoms. Sonja let go of the serape and bent down. She touched the tops of the buds, and they stretched their petals wide, revealing scarlet-colored centers. She smiled and ran through the center of the bloom, her fingers brushing the tops of the flowers. The buds opened, revealing a crimson river flowing against the veined cracks of the dry earth.

Sonja danced through the flowers, coaxing the buds to open as Yolanda and Hasik collected handfuls of the flowers and Hasik wove them into Wela's serape. The butterflies and bumblebees drank hungrily. Ghita tried to weave a blossom into Sonja's hair, but Sonja glanced back at Yolanda nervously and took the flower from Ghita, tucking it in herself.

"Ghita likes her." Hasik leaned in. "But that doesn't mean you and Ghita can't be friends."

Yolanda wasn't sure what to think anymore.

Thirty-five

AS THE group made their way through the wildflower bloom, they passed around the water bottles. Wela stirred and asked for a sip of water. Sonja helped her drink.

Rosalind Franklin sat down and refused to keep walking. Ghita picked the dog up and placed her on Wela's lap. The serape sank in, but it held. Wela stroked the top of Rosalind Franklin's head, and the dog's eyelids began to close.

"How was it your fault?" Ghita asked, taking a sip of water. "With what happened to Violeta?"

A look of sadness crept across Wela's face as she continued with her story.

I ran all the way home to tell Mami and Papá about the

fire. They were already filling buckets when I got back. They had smelled the smoke. Mami and I filled buckets of water, while Papá and Raúl rode back and forth on horses, trying to keep it from moving toward the house.

"What were those girls doing? Something's not right," Mami said. "I saw Cynthia Purty running away."

"Nothing, Mami. It was nothing." But I couldn't shake the way they had surrounded my sister. What would have happened if I hadn't been there to stop them?

Mami heaved a large bucket onto the back of the trailer. "Did they start this fire?"

I chewed the inside of my lip.

"Josefa! I know you aren't telling me something. I can feel it." Mami waited for me to answer, and when I didn't, she threw her hands up. "Go and get Vi! She needs to get out here and help." Mami wiped her hands across her apron.

I didn't move.

"Jo, go and get your sister right now!" Mami yelled.

"I can't, Mami."

"¿Por qué no?"

"She left." Tears formed in the corners of my eyes.

"Left? Where did she go?" Mami asked. "She knows the plan when there's a fire."

"She left to be with Benjamín," I said.

Mami's hands flew to her face, smudging black soot on her

cheeks. Her hands shook as I told her about the suitcase and the bus ticket.

Mami thought that was all I was hiding from her.

Papá and Raúl rode frantically up the orchard.

"It's coming across the river. We need to wet down the house," Papá said.

"Papá?" I said. He should know too.

"Basta!" Mami shook her head. This was not the time to tell him about Violeta. "As long as your sister is safe on a bus, we will worry about her later," Mami whispered as we filled buckets of water.

The air was thick with black smoke, and my eyes burned. We filled bucket after bucket from the well, lining them up for Papá and Raúl to collect. Mami and I soaked the wraparound porch and my favorite tree by the bay window.

Then the winds changed.

It pushed the line of fire closer and closer to our house.

Papá and Raúl rode up on the horses and called out, "Load up the buckets! We need more water!"

They rode back and forth across the orchard, dumping water along the perimeter of our house while Mami and I continued to fill buckets.

My heart ached for Violeta. How could she have abandoned us? Would she ever come back? Would I ever see her again?

Finally Papá and Raúl rode up, their eyes red and cheeks smudged with soot.

"It's no use." Papá rubbed his eyes. "It's going to burn all the way to the edge of the property. It already made it to the casita. It's all we can do to keep it from coming to the house."

We spent the rest of the evening wetting the house with buckets of water in hopes it wouldn't catch fire. The fire inched closer and closer. Raúl and I ran up and down the stairs with buckets and poured them over the roof.

"It's going to be okay," Raúl said, patting my back. "Papá and Mami will rebuild. You know how this land is. It always comes back."

"I'm fine," I said.

"No you're not. You're sad," Raúl said.

"I am not."

"You are." He dumped a bucket of water out the window. "I can feel it."

I shook my head at him. "It's nothing, Raúl."

"It's not nothing. It's a horrible ache in my chest."

The fire crept closer and closer until finally the winds changed and the fire moved south along the property, burning every pecan tree in sight, all the way to the butte.

Then, a low rumble in the distance gave us hope. Maybe the rains would come.

The rains did come and put out the fire, dampening the gray-black smoke hanging in the air. It rained all night long and into the next morning. I was grateful the fire was out, but my chest still ached.

It wasn't until the next afternoon that Papá called up the stairs. "Vi!"

Mami broke down as she told Papá that Violeta was gone.

His face went gray when she said his name.

Benjamín.

I was sure she had made it to the bus station.

She was halfway to Dallas.

I knew in my heart she had begun a new life with Benjamín.

We were not prepared for what we found.

Two days after the fire, Papá found her at the edge of the property, next to the family cemetery, the suitcase tucked by her side. She lay underneath the very last pecan tree, high on the butte. She wasn't burned, not at all, but she was covered in black ash. Soot stained her nostrils.

The sheriff said she must have fainted from the smoke. The smoke must have been so thick, he told my papá, that she couldn't see. Just a few yards farther and she would have made it over the butte, down the other side, and would have escaped the fire.

Mami and Papá were devastated. Raúl was devastated.

I was devastated.

If only I had said something sooner. If I had told them about what those girls did. If I had told someone earlier, maybe Papá and Raúl could have ridden out to her.

Maybe they could have saved her.

Maybe she wouldn't have died.

Thirty-six

"SHE'S lost so much." Sonja wiped her eyes.

Yolanda pushed a lock of limp gray hair out of Wela's face. Her eyes were finally closed and she was resting again. Yolanda's heart ached for Wela. Her sister, her daughter, her husband. How did she go on? How did Wela find a way to keep moving forward after all those losses? Yolanda had been devastated by the death of Welo. It ate at her every day, pushing her away from her friends and family, swallowing her into a lonely cocoon. It seemed Wela handled these losses with such strength. But then again, she could see the pain in Wela's eyes, the way she looked into the distance like she was trying to close herself off from feeling it all the way too.

Ghita grabbed one side of the serape and Sonja grabbed the other, pulling Wela along the center of the riverbed through the crimson blossoms. Yolanda, Hasik, and Rosalind Franklin walked behind.

"She still hasn't told us what's in the box." Hasik kicked the toe of his shoe over the red wildflower bloom. The odor from the flowers was sour. Wela clutched the metal box in her lap even as she slept.

"She will," Sonja said. "She'll tell us."

A tan-colored snake with diamond-patterned scales slithered between the blossoms in front of Yolanda and Hasik. Its bright pointy head waved back and forth menacingly.

"S-S-Sonja," Yolanda managed to squeak out. "Snake."

Sonja and Ghita whipped around. Wela floated between them on the serape.

The snake shook the end of its tail, making a rattling sound.

The sound sent shivers up Yolanda's spine. She knew that sound well. Rosalind Franklin darted toward it, barking, the hackles down her back raised. Yolanda snatched her up as she wiggled and snarled.

Another snake slithered from the blossoms and headed toward Sonja and Ghita.

They froze, their eyes wide.

Sonja pulled a machete out of her backpack and held it

in ready position. The snake slithered closer, then raised its head and rattled its tail. Sonja gripped the machete tighter, her knuckles turning white.

"Don't move," Ghita said between clenched teeth. She reached into her pocket and pulled out the tiny punji flute.

She began to play.

It was an eerie, slow tune, and at first it didn't seem to do anything at all. But as she continued playing the song, the snakes calmed and lifted their diamond-shaped heads off the ground, swaying back and forth.

"What are they doing?" Yolanda asked.

"Stay still." Hasik held his arm out protectively. "Nani—she taught Ghita."

Ghita continued to play the song, and although the snakes seemed calm, they were still within striking distance.

Rosalind Franklin barked, spooking the snake closest to Sonja. It reared back, ready to strike at her knee.

"Stay still!" Ghita commanded, her hands shaking.

She dropped the flute at her feet.

Right in front of the snakes.

The pair of snakes began move erratically again, and Ghita pinched her eyes closed and reached one hand to the ground. Her fingers curled around the punji when Rosalind Franklin began to bark again.

"Quiet!" Sonja hissed. Ghita froze.

The snakes pressed in on Sonja and Ghita again.

They got closer and closer.

Yolanda held Rosalind Franklin tight, but she kept squirming, making it impossible to keep a hold of her fat body. She wiggled free and fell to the ground barking. She righted herself and dashed at the snakes.

The snakes scattered apart.

One turned around and slithered toward Hasik and Yolanda.

Hasik backed away.

Then he stumbled and fell backward.

The snake reared its head back and sank its fangs deep into Hasik's ankle.

Hasik screamed.

"Hasik!" Ghita cried, reaching for her brother. She looked as though she wanted to run to him but was trapped by the snake between them.

Yolanda ran to Hasik, and without thinking she peeled the snake's head out of his ankle, flung it to the ground, and scrambled away.

Her hands shaking, Ghita began to play the slow, eerie tune again. And the other snake began to calm, swaying back and forth.

But the snake that had struck Hasik kept its eyes on him. It rattled its tail again.

Hasik crawled away, his eyes wide and terror-filled. He breathed heavily.

As Ghita continued to play and the snake calmed, Sonja tiptoed away. She made her way toward Hasik, who was propped up on his elbows, his face pale and sweaty. Blood dripped down his ankle. The snake lifted its head, threatening to strike again.

"Help!" Hasik cried.

Sonja sent a small swarm of bees toward the snake. The snake thrashed back and forth as the bees swarmed its head. It quickly slithered back into the flowers and disappeared.

Beads of sweat gathered over Hasik's upper lip, and he fell back, clutching his bleeding ankle. His lips were purple.

Sonja walked behind the calm snake as Ghita played. It slowly lowered its head and began to slither away. Sonja bent down and examined the markings as it went. Then she looked at Yolanda. "These are venomous."

Thirty-seven

HASIK lay in the bottom of the riverbed clutching his ankle. It was starting to swell, the skin taut and shiny, and drops of blood dripped from two small holes, darkening his white sock.

"Does it hurt?" Yolanda looked him over.

Hasik's face was pale. He nodded and lay back.

"Hasik!" Ghita ran to his side, leaving Wela on her blanket hovering nearby.

"Take off his belt," Sonja instructed. Ghita did as she was told, then handed it to Sonja.

"Stay still," Yolanda said, her hand resting on his chest. "The more you move or panic, the faster the venom will travel into your system. It's the same with the bees."

Yolanda held Hasik's leg steady as Sonja tightened the belt below his knee.

Hasik cried out.

"Don't move." Yolanda sat back on her heels and brushed the wild hair from her face. "What do we do now?"

"I don't know," Sonja whispered. "I was always told if a rattlesnake gets you, you have to get to the hospital as fast as possible for antivenom."

There was no way they were going to get antivenom out here. Yolanda remembered something Hasik had said earlier. "Hasik said your Nani was a snake charmer. I'm sure she got bitten, right?"

"Yes. Loads of times, but not by rattlesnakes." Ghita stood, her brow furrowed and eyes wild. She paced in a circle around her brother, wringing her hands.

Yolanda stood and placed both of her hands on Ghita's shoulders, steadying her. "What did she do for the bites? Did she put something on them?"

"She . . . She . . . had me make a poultice for her one time. It was some plants . . . I don't know. I don't know—we don't have all those things way out here. That was in India!" Ghita cried.

"Hasik has turmeric," Yolanda said. Hasik's eyes were closed. Yolanda shook him awake. "Hasik!"

His eyelids fluttered open and he cried out. He tried to sit up.

Yolanda pushed his shoulders to the ground. "Try not to move," she said gently. "What kinds of plants can you use for snakebites?"

Hasik moaned again and closed his eyes. Yolanda pinched him hard on the bridge of his nose.

"Ow!" he cried.

"Wake up and tell me. Plants for snakebites. Go!"

"Turmeric . . . uh, p-p-plantains, prickly pear . . . There was . . . echinacea a little ways back. It's mostly dried out, but it might help."

"What does it look like?"

"It's sort of cone-shaped—pink flowers." His eyelids fluttered.

Sonja left to gather the plants as Yolanda knelt next to Hasik and dug the turmeric out of his pocket. She handed it to Ghita, who went to find a flat stone to crush it. Every time he shut his eyes, Yolanda pinched him awake.

"You are not allowed to fall asleep." She gripped his hand tight.

"Afraid you'll miss me, huh?" he said weakly, and smiled. The smile that used to bother her, but not anymore. The color was draining from his lips, and his teeth began to chatter. "My leg really hurts," he said.

"You're going to be fine," she said, but she gripped his hand a little tighter.

When his eyes closed again, she knew she had to do something. She let go of his hand and moved down toward his ankle, holding it between her hands. He winced when she moved it. The swelling was moving up his calf to his knee.

Rosalind Franklin pressed her paws into Hasik's chest and licked the dampness from his pale cheek.

Yolanda glanced at the cut on her dog's hind leg. It was completely healed, with a thin pink scar.

She considered it.

No.

She pulled Rosalind Franklin in close and examined the cut more closely. It was perfectly healed.

It had been only a day.

She brushed her hand along her shoulder. The teeth marks were gone.

Impossible.

She looked around. Ghita was crushing the turmeric into a pulp, and Sonja had returned with the dried-out echinacea. Sonja touched the centers of the dried cone-flowers and they immediately brightened, the brown petals turning a vibrant pink and the green stems rejuvenating with life.

Yolanda bit her lip. It was worth a shot.

Holding Hasik's ankle in her hands, she drew her face close, pursed her lips, and blew onto the punctures. The air felt cool across her lips. A steady stream of blood poured out of the wound, dripping dark burgundy splotches into the brown dust below. His ankle quickly warmed between her hands as she pressed gently on the swelling. More blood poured out. The swelling started to go down as more and more blood flowed from the holes. She was too afraid to release the belt around his calf.

Ghita and Sonja came over with the poultice cupped in their hands. Yolanda ripped a triangle of fabric from the bottom of her T-shirt, soaked it with water, and plopped the greenish-orange poultice in the center. The swelling was already going down. She quickly wrapped the shirt around his ankle before anyone could see. Hasik winced at first and then relaxed, his eyes still closed.

"He doesn't look good." Ghita bit her thumbnail.

"He's going to be okay," Yolanda said. She was sure she had felt it. The coolness across her lips. It was just as Margaret Purty had described when Violeta healed her arm in Wela's story. Yolanda had felt it too when she'd healed Rosalind Franklin, and the blisters on her thumbs. The healing coolness.

"How can you say that?" Ghita threw her hands up and paced in a circle again. "It was a venomous snake! This may not work at all."

"It will," Yolanda said more firmly. It had to work.

"It will," Wela repeated, a twinkle in her eye. She was still hovering on the serape. She must have woken during the commotion. Wela sat up and looked around. "Are we ready to go, then?"

"Yes." Yolanda picked up her backpack and slung it over her shoulder.

"We can't leave him here," Ghita cried.

"Of course not," Yolanda said. "You stay here with him until we get back."

"We need to get him to a hospital." Ghita's eyes were full of worry and panic.

Yolanda turned back and held her arms wide. "Look where we are. There are no hospitals here, Ghita!"

"He'll be all right," Wela said, nodding.

Sonja looked torn. "Are you sure?" She looked from Ghita to Wela.

Wela nodded.

Sonja flung a backpack over her shoulder. "We have to get Wela to the tree first. Then we can get him home."

"Sonja, don't leave us." Ghita pressed her palms together. She was begging.

Sonja sighed. "It'll be okay. I have to help Wela, and then we'll come back for you. I promise."

"Everything will be set right when we get to the tree—right, Wela?" Yolanda said.

Wela nodded and pointed a finger to the sky. "*Sí, mija.*"

"Let's go, then," Yolanda said, starting toward the serape.

"Wait." Hasik's eyelids fluttered open. "Come here a second."

Yolanda knelt down beside him and gripped his clammy palm.

"You'll come back, right?" he said.

Yolanda nodded. She didn't want to leave him. Not at all. But she knew he'd be okay. She'd felt it.

And Wela. She needed to get to the tree.

Hasik closed his eyes and groaned. "I did this on purpose, you know. So you'd feel sorry for me." He grinned, and Yolanda felt her insides warm. She suddenly wanted him to know how she felt.

"I promise I'll come back," she whispered in his ear. "And it's not maybe anymore."

A smile flashed across his face, even though his eyes were closed. She gripped his hand one last time and stood, leaving him with a faint smile on his face. She pinched her lips together to keep from smiling. She was glad she'd told him.

Wela rode quietly on the humming serape as Sonja and Yolanda each took a side and walked out of the riverbed to the base of the butte. The pecan tree was at the top, its limbs twisting in the wind.

Hasik lay on the ground with his eyes closed and his leg wrapped up in the juicy poultice. Rosalind Franklin rested her head on his shoulder, and Ghita sat next to him, nervously biting her thumbnail.

Thirty-eight

SONJA pointed out the trail they needed to take to the top of the butte. The enormous trunk of the pecan tree emerged from the earth as its dark skeletal arms reached in every direction. The sisters hummed along the rocky trail, the bees and butterflies buzzing underneath the colorful serape. Yolanda gazed back at the dry riverbed down below. From there, the vein-like pattern in the earth appeared etched on, broken up only by the crimson river of blossoms. She looked again for the house, but beyond the riverbed was never-ending grass that had grown even taller. She spotted the rickety bridge where Hasik had given her the orange flower, and it looked tiny from up here.

She felt for the flower.

It was gone.

Hasik.

What if it hadn't worked?

She looked to Wela, who was asleep again. The creases in her face seemed to deepen the closer they got to the tree. Her dull hair hung lank off the back of the serape.

But Wela needed her.

The clouds in the deep blue sky were beginning to darken as the wind whistled through the desert grasses. Yolanda twisted a curl of her hair around her finger. What if they didn't make it in time? The thought made her nauseous.

Her hand brushed her shoulder, and the skin was smooth and taut. She thought of Rosalind Franklin's cut and Hasik's leg.

What if she had healed them? Could she have healed herself, too?

The possibility sent an electric surge through her body. It was exciting and yet terrifying at the same time.

What if?

The more she thought about it, the more jittery and dizzy she felt. Her heart skipped a beat in her chest.

Then she thought of Violeta and Mamá.

The weight of the responsibility of their gifts sat heavy on her shoulders.

"You like your bees . . . ," Yolanda asked Sonja, "don't you?"

Sonja walked ahead, pulling the fringe of the serape. She turned slightly before answering and chewed the inside of her cheek as two bees flew around the limp red flowers in her braid. Even sunburned with dry, cracked lips, she was beautiful.

"They're okay." Sonja shrugged.

"Just . . . okay?"

Sonja climbed over a large boulder. "To be perfectly honest, I was scared when they came." She pulled the serape around it and waited for Yolanda to catch up. "I don't like bees."

"Really?" Yolanda grasped the rough boulder with her fingertips. "But you seem to be doing fine with them." She pulled herself up and over, landing with a *thud*.

"Fine?" Sonja scoffed. "The only person who would talk to me after they showed up was Ghita. Even you stopped talking to me. Eli Jensen's mom threw a fit at the camping club meeting after one of the bees stung him. It was awful. I thought I'd never live that down. I've had to incorporate them into my daily life, pretending I'm interested in them for science projects so no one knows the truth about me. Same as Wela studying the butterflies so no one knew the truth about her. And with all that, the town still hates us and calls us *bru*—" She stopped herself before she said the word. "And never mind the fact that they sting you and you almost die." Sonja puffed out her chest. "So, no, I guess I don't like them."

Yolanda was surprised by this. Sonja didn't like her bees? How could that be? "But it's your gift—and Wela helps you." Her feet slid on the rocks, and she gripped the fringe of the serape to keep from falling.

"The plant stuff is pretty cool. Like how Wela showed me how to make the prickly pear fruits come." Sonja reached out and touched the tip of a dried stalk of lavender. It sprang to life, its purple blossoms opening and emitting a calming aroma.

"That's amazing," Yolanda whispered. She hadn't realized all that Sonja was capable of with her gift. She was getting better at it.

Sonja glanced back. "I started trying at Wela's urging."

Yolanda felt a tickle on her finger.

She immediately let go of the serape, her heart in her throat.

A bee had climbed onto her hand.

She froze.

"Wela is trying to help me, but it's hard." Sonja waved her hand around haphazardly. "Any time I am not fully present and paying attention, the bees can get out of control."

Yolanda moved her hand back near the fringe and let the bee crawl underneath the serape. She let out her breath all at once. That was close.

"Honestly, I don't really like having them. Wela said one day I'll appreciate the gift, but right now I wish I were just ordinary."

That word stuck in Yolanda's throat.

Ordinary? But she was ordinary.

She gulped.

Or maybe she wasn't anymore.

They came upon rows of prickly pear cactus. They weren't the usual green ones that Hasik had foraged for them, but a deep lavender covered with bright yellow flowers.

Hasik would love these, Yolanda thought.

Yolanda checked to make sure Wela was still asleep. "How did you and Ghita . . . happen?"

Sonja brushed a stray hair out of her face, disturbing a bee in her braid. It flew a loop around her head before settling back into a shadow of her hair. "We needed each other," she said. "Actually, we needed you. But you weren't there, so we found each other. We started hanging out, and then we happened to like each other more than friends . . ."

"I know. I know." Yolanda rolled her eyes. "It's so not fair—you got your first kiss way before me."

"Oh brother. First kisses are so super awkward. I didn't know where to put my lips or my hands. Right before we kissed, I was so nervous I thought I was going to barf. It was all kinds of weird. Now, second and third kisses, that's when things get better." Sonja smiled.

"So that kiss in the hallway was . . . ?"

Sonja held up four fingers. "Number four."

"You really like her, don't you?"

Sonja sighed, her eyes shining. "I do. She makes my knees wobble and my hands shake. She is what I think people are looking for when they write romantic songs and poems. She's thoughtful and kind, smart. . . . Don't get me wrong, she drives me crazy too, but there's something about her . . ."

"What happened, then? Why have you been so . . . ?"

Sonja sighed again. "I don't know. I guess my feelings are a mess." Sonja ran her fingers along the dried desert grasses. Under her touch, the blades turned a deep green and softened with life. "I messed things up with her."

"It's not complicated." Yolanda plucked a bit of the green grass and rolled it between her fingers. "If you like her, then be nice to her."

Sonja glanced over her shoulder and rolled her eyes. "Says the girl who is nice to no one."

"I'm nice," Yolanda protested, and then she laughed.

"Okay, I'm not that nice. All I'm saying is if you like Ghita, then date her, kiss her, like her. Why does it have to be so complicated?"

"To be honest, I was—I am worried about what you think. She's your best friend. Or *was* your best friend, and I care about not hurting you."

That news hit Yolanda in the chest, and the words left her. It never seemed that either of them really cared about her feelings. It was nice to hear Sonja say that. Then suddenly she felt guilty.

"Don't worry about me." Yolanda shrugged. "I'm fine with it. Whatever is going to make the two of you happy." And she realized that was how she really felt. Sonja and Ghita liked each other, and even though that left her out, she wanted them both to be happy.

"Well, what's Dad going to say? What if he doesn't understand?"

"Dad will be fine," Yolanda said. "He loves you." She wrapped an arm around her sister. "And if I have to, I'll make sure he understands."

Sonja smiled. "Thanks, Yo."

Yolanda hugged her sister. She heard the familiar buzzing of the bees and stood quickly. "Sorry," she said, backing away. "The bees."

"Yeah, we don't need you getting stung out here."

Yolanda glanced down the trail, and Sonja noticed.

"I hope Hasik is okay," Sonja said. Then a wry smile came over her face. "You know, Hasik likes you."

"Oh, no," Yolanda protested, shaking her head. "I don't think he—" Her palms began to sweat. Were they that obvious?

"Yes he does. He always talks about how smart you are. He has a major crush on you. He came all this way, out in the desert—for you."

Yolanda thought of him lying on the riverbed and hoped she was right and had helped him.

"Wait a second! You like him too, don't you?" Sonja broke out into a huge grin. "I can see it on your face."

"I don't know—I don't know," Yolanda said quickly. Her cheeks burned.

"You DO like him!"

Yolanda's heart thumped in her chest. She did like Hasik. He was kind to her. And smart and funny. And Sonja had shared so much about Ghita. It was time to be honest with herself. And with Sonja. "Yeah, I like him," she said finally.

Sonja clapped her hands together. "Yay!" she said happily.

Yolanda laughed.

Wela stirred on the serape and opened her eyes. Her

skin was gray and matched her dull hair. "Water," she said.

Yolanda helped her sip from the water bottle.

"*Mijas*, we are almost there. I can feel it," Wela said. "It's time to tell you about the tree."

Thirty-nine

ONCE I told Mami and Papá about what Cynthia and Fiona did, they demanded justice. For months they fought with the sheriff, begging him to do something. Anything.

Mami even confronted Pastor Jones. But nothing ever came of it.

It never does in a town where everyone calls you a bruja.

One by one, like a plague on our land, the burned trees fell. This tree, then that one. Papá and Raúl cut them into pieces and sold the firewood. It sapped my parents' savings. We had little food and no money that winter. The Rodríguez pecans were no more.

Violeta's tree was the only one left, standing tall and proud on the butte.

Mami rocked in her chair by the window, staring into the dying orchard, hoping maybe we got it all wrong. Maybe the orchard wasn't dying. Maybe Vi wasn't gone.

Her fingers were red and raw from pulling at her skin. She would whisper to herself over and over again, "It's a strange land, for a strange family."

The following spring, the desert air was crisp as the winds blew in and I led Mami outside to the porch swing for some fresh air. She was swinging back and forth, her mouth agape.

I followed her gaze to Violeta's tree.

The family tree.

It still stood proud and tall. But it wasn't bare and black as it had been the entire winter.

It was green.

Violeta's tree had bloomed.

Raúl and I rode out there and sat underneath it, surrounded by the gravestones of our family.

He breathed in the air from the tree, leaned back and crossed his arms behind his head. "This is the best I've felt in a while." He gazed up at the overhanging branches. "It's like she's here with us, isn't it?"

I glanced around, shaded by the lush green-and-white beauty surrounding us. Long chains of lime-green buds dangled above. I felt lucky to be able see this. I felt lucky this one had survived.

"Can we come here every day?" Raúl spread out his arms. "I feel so amazing here."

It was her tree.

I knew in my gut she had healed it.

Whenever we went back to the sadness of the house, it swallowed us whole. The grief wove itself into the walls, the floors, and our existence like an insidious infection.

It hurt us all.

But especially Raúl.

His eyes darkened and his face paled whenever we walked up the steps to the house. It was like it was making him sick.

So every day that spring and through the summer, Raúl and I rode out to the tree and spent as much time as we could there. It was the happiest we could be, sitting under her tree.

By autumn, the leaves were golden yellow and the outer shells of the nuts had begun to split open, ready to harvest. Raúl climbed up the rough, thick branches and shook the tree, raining hard brown shells all around me.

He jumped down and helped me gather the nuts into a large sack.

"How much do you know about the family?" Raúl said. "¿Quién es?" He dug a stick into a dust-covered V in the gravestone. "Who is this?"

The name read VALENTINA RODRÍGUEZ-DOMÍNGUEZ. And underneath, TELEPATÍA.

"I think that's Mami's sister, Valentina." I grabbed a handful of nuts from the ground and placed them into my sack.

"What was her gift?"

"Telepatía. It means she could read minds."

"Do you think mine will ever come?" Raúl crouched down in front of Violeta's gravestone, raised a thumb, and cleaned the dust from the letters of her name.

I shrugged. I wasn't sure. He was only eleven. "Mine came around twelve." I sat down. A butterfly perched on my fingertip, and I gently blew on its wings, letting it catch a puff of air and fly away. I picked up one of the shiny brown nuts and held it in my palm. I tapped the top and it burst open, revealing the pecan inside.

"Don't you think it's strange the tree made nuts?" Raúl asked. He was swinging from a lower limb.

I placed the nut in my mouth. "Why do you say that?"

"Because usually they need to be cross-pollinated. Pecan trees don't pollinate themselves. And all the other trees are dead." He wrapped his legs around the branch.

His words didn't matter as I chewed the nut. It was the sweetest pecan I had ever tasted.

"Raúl, you have to try this," I said, handing him the other half.

That afternoon we rode back to the house, our arms over-loaded with bags and bags of pecans, the warm autumn sun at our backs. We were thrilled.

These nuts would save the orchard.

We brought them to Papá.

His eyes darkened and his jaw set tight. He snatched the sacks and threw them straight into the fire. "Never, ever go to that tree again." His eyes glistened with the tears he tried to hold back. "¿Entendido? Never."

I couldn't understand why he would react that way. He should have been pleased that we were going to save the orchard. Raúl said it was because Papá was so devastated over losing Violeta that seeing the orchard blooming again and life going on without her was too much for him to bear.

Forty

AS THEY continued to climb, Yolanda's breath quickened. Sonja was in the front, pulling the serape, and Yolanda stayed in the back, carefully avoiding the bees. As Wela slept, Yolanda had a foreboding feeling they were running out of time. If Wela died before they got her to the tree, Yolanda would never forgive herself. She found herself checking Wela over and over again, making sure she was still breathing.

"You know, Yo, I wish I were like you." Sonja picked her way through a thick grove of ocotillo. Bright red flowers emerged from the tops of the long arms, emitting an earthy vanilla aroma.

Yolanda raised an eyebrow. "Me?"

"You are so smart and independent. You don't care what anyone else thinks about you. I would have never had the courage to take Wela here on my own."

Sonja's words surprised her. "I'm not on my own. You, Ghita, and Hasik came." Then it hit her. She'd needed them on this journey. "I wouldn't have made it this far without you guys."

"Maybe, but you were determined to do it on your own."

"That was a little stupid," Yolanda admitted. "I would have never been able to get Wela here without you and your bees. I would have had to give up way back there." A bee crawled onto the back of Yolanda's hand and she swatted it away quickly. "And all your outdoor skills—I would have never made it."

Sonja laughed, but her eyes were sad. They trudged up the trail for a few moments in silence.

"Do you ever wonder about Welo?" Sonja said. "Like where is he? Is he with Mamá? What happened to *him*—after he took his last breath? Where did *he* go?"

Those questions made Yolanda dizzy. She didn't like to think about those kinds of things. She didn't want to look at Sonja either, and kept her eyes down, but before she could stop herself, the words came pouring out. "I really miss him."

They walked for a few more moments in silence.

"Me too."

Three days before Welo died, Yolanda had stayed in the library all day long, filling up the final pages of a third spiral notebook. Dad had asked her to come home early that day. He wanted to spend time together, as a family. But Yolanda, too engrossed in her work, did not come home until dinner.

Well after dark, when everyone was asleep, Yolanda crept into Welo's bedroom. Wela slept next to him, and Sonja snored softly on a small pallet of blankets she had made on the floor.

Yolanda smoothed the yellow serape over his chest and whispered, "I didn't find a cure today, Welo, but I'll keep looking."

Welo's eyelids fluttered. He grabbed her hand and squeezed. "Stay with me, *mija*."

Yolanda kissed Welo's hand. "I want to, but I've got work to do."

He gripped her hand a bit tighter. He glanced at Wela, who was sleeping beside him. "I know you don't care about it now, but I need you to finish my work. Figure out the gift. If we can explain it to the world, then maybe they will understand. People won't treat Wela this way anymore. Or you and Sonja when your gifts come."

Yolanda held up her hand and shook her head. "Welo, I am going to find a cure for you. To make you better. You can finish your *own* work—when you are better."

"But, Yo—please." His eyes were desperate and pleading. "I want a good life for you."

"I know, Welo." Yolanda had patted him on the arm. "I'm close. I just need to keep looking." She closed the door behind her and continued her research in her bedroom.

Two days later, Dad told her the doctors were changing Welo's pain medication. Things were not looking good. "He doesn't have much longer," he had said.

With that news, Yolanda hopped on her bike and rode away furiously, toward the college. She couldn't look at Welo and tell him she had failed.

She had to find the cure. She had to save him.

But she didn't.

Welo died that afternoon. He died while she had six health magazines splayed out on the table. He took his last breaths as she jotted down notes about things that didn't cure cancer.

Wela was there.

Dad was there.

Sonja was there.

Yolanda wasn't.

"How did he go?" Yolanda asked as they marched up

the mountain, the dry grasses scratching her shins. "How did he die?" Her voice cracked. She had never wanted to know before this. It had been too hard to even think about.

Sonja's face grew solemn. "Peacefully," she said. "It was quiet. He asked to go outside, and so we propped him on the porch swing and covered him with a blanket. I lay next to him, my head on his lap. I sang him a song. Dad and Wela sat on the floor next to him and held his hands. That's all he wanted in the end, to be with us."

Yolanda's insides twisted painfully as she pictured the scene. It sounded so achingly beautiful. "I can't believe I missed it." The guilt overwhelmed her, and she couldn't breathe. Why couldn't she face the truth?

Sonja's eyes glistened. "He knew that it would be hard for you. You were determined to save him. He knew that."

Yolanda hadn't wanted to miss his last moments. That wasn't her plan. Her plan was to save his life so they could have many more moments together. So he could teach her everything he knew about science and genetics and life. So that he could finish his work.

But that didn't happen.

"I was so mad at Mrs. Patel." Yolanda wiped away her tears. "I was so mad at her for not being there. I was mad she didn't save him."

"Her own mother was sick," Sonja said. "She had to go."

"Hasik told me." Yolanda shook her head. "I didn't know. That's why Ghita left too."

Sonja nodded. "It was hard for Ghita when she came back. She lost her grandmother and you, her best friend. She didn't know how to talk to you about it."

"She disappeared. She left me."

Sonja's head snapped up. "No one left you, Yo," she said, narrowing her eyes. "You. You were the one who left everyone."

Yolanda stopped, Sonja's words hitting her. Sonja was right.

She had closed everyone off. She'd closed herself off before he died. When death was the only outcome, she'd hidden in her books and research, not willing to face the reality of what was going to happen.

They walked for a few more moments in silence.

"You and Welo are a lot alike," Sonja said. "Always wanting to be alone."

Yolanda hadn't thought much of it before, but she liked to be alone. It was her way of focusing and dealing with the world, taking it in. Coping. She could close the door and cry and not have to answer to anyone.

"Do you hate me?" Sonja asked. "Because of Ghita?"

"What a strange question. No, of course not."

"Do you hate Ghita?"

"No."

"Then why does it feel like you do? Since Welo died, you treat us like we wronged you. At first I thought it was your grieving thing. Wela said everyone grieves in their own way, but now I'm beginning to think it's something else." Sonja's freckled cheeks were pale, exhaustion behind her eyes. "Is it because . . . you know . . . we like each other? Because I didn't mean for it to happen. It wasn't on purpose."

"It's not that." Yolanda knew she needed to say the truth. She needed to finally say what was bothering her about Ghita and Sonja.

"What, then?" Sonja's mouth was open, but there was worry behind her eyes. It was clear that she cared what Yolanda thought.

Yolanda closed her eyes. "You both left me. You are both leaving me."

"What?" Sonja's brow furrowed. "*You* abandoned us. *You* abandoned Welo!"

"I was trying to save him!" Yolanda yelled.

"But he couldn't be saved." Sonja shook her head at the ground. "And you missed out on the little life he had left."

Yolanda's chest ached with grief. Hearing the truth that she knew in her heart out loud was so painful.

"We didn't mean to leave you out, Ghita and me." Sonja

stopped and tried to put her arm around Yolanda. "We thought you wanted to be alone."

"I did. I did want to be alone," Yolanda said. She felt like her chest was cracking open, the grief pouring out of her. "But I don't want to be alone anymore."

Forty-one

Wela woke again, shaky and weak. Even the wings of the butterflies in her hair seemed as though they were growing listless. Yolanda helped her sit up and take a sip of water. Then she continued her story.

A few months later, another letter arrived from Benjamín. I snuck it from the mailbox and opened it before anyone else saw it.

Mi amor Violeta,
I am heartbroken you never came. I know what you must think about me, but I promise I had not planned to fall in love with you. It just happened. I hope one day you can forgive me for not telling you the truth about my work.

After you did not meet me in Dallas, I decided to go to war. There is no point in my life without you in it, so I am writing to you from a ship somewhere in the middle of the ocean. I'm on my way to fight the Nazis.

Please forgive me. I cannot live and I cannot die knowing you are angry with me.

Te amo,
Benjamín

I had to write him. I had to tell him what happened to her. I told him my sister, his love, was gone.

He was devastated, of course, like the rest of us. We wrote back and forth like that, in secret. No one in the family knew I was writing to him. That would have been a betrayal to them. And through those letters I learned Benjamín loved my sister very much.

Over the harsh desert winter, Mami rocked back and forth in her rocking chair and stared through the window at the pecan tree on the butte, never saying much at all. Raúl had grown sad, like the rest of us, but this was more. It was as if he held the sadness right inside his heart like a living, breathing thing.

I couldn't bring myself to look at the tree anymore. It was too much. When the first buds began to sprout in early spring, Papá packed up the house and moved us. We had to leave before the orchard came back to life.

As we left, my papá repeated Mami's words under his breath. "It's a strange land."

We moved to a nearby town, where Papá and Mami opened up a small grocery store and made a meager living.

They were never happy again. Not really.

As the years passed by and I grew up, we went through the motions of life, but we were never the same. A family never is after a tragedy like that. As soon as I was eighteen, I went to college. I came home a few times a year to visit with them, but it was always Mami rocking in her chair and Papá never saying much at all. Sometimes Raúl and I would sneak over to the pecan orchard and ride to her tree, enveloping ourselves in the beauty of it all. The orchard had finally started to come back to life after the fire, but Papá didn't want to hear about it. Raúl went to fight in Korea in 1951, and shortly after he left, Papá died first and then Mami a few months after. Raúl wrote me and said it was because they were left alone with each other, living in sadness.

Many years later, in 1964, after I gave birth to your Mamá, Welo and I were living in an old apartment in Albuquerque by the university when a package came. It was addressed to me, Josefa Rodríguez. It was the will and testament of my brother, Raúl.

Dear Josefa,

If you have received this letter, it means I am

gone. There isn't much left to be said. I don't think I ever recovered from the loss of our sister. And the war did me no favors. I've tried to hang on, but I couldn't. I'm so sorry.

Her tree is standing, tall and proud, just like her. It blooms every spring and drops the sweetest nuts in autumn. The rest of the orchard is trying to come back, but I could hardly leave the house, let alone take care of it on my own.

I'm leaving the orchard to you. Maybe you won't want it. Maybe you will sell it, but I hope you find it in your heart to keep it. Papá and Mami are buried there, next to Violeta, as they wanted. All I ask is that you have me buried there too, per the family tradition. Maybe one day you can bring it back to life and it will be fruitful again. I wish we could have seen each other more, but the nightmares kept me home most of the time.

I am at peace now.

Te amo,
Raúl

For many years, I thought Papá had sold the orchard, but he hadn't. He had given it to my brother in secret. It had been in Mami's family for so long there was no way she would have wanted anyone else to have it.

Raúl died thirteen years after he came home from Korea—shell shock they said. But I knew the nightmares filled his house, his life. He never recovered from Violeta's death or his time in the war. It ate at him, bit by bit, every day.

And so your Welo, your mamá, and I moved out of our tiny apartment to the orchard. It was an absolute mess, and you couldn't really call it an orchard anymore. There were a few young pecan trees trying to sprout, but the house was in shambles. I knew with some time and care we could bring it back to life. We spent years fixing the outside, painting the shutters and working the land. I became good at helping the young pecan trees grow and coaxing the blood sage to return.

We had a mostly happy life.

Wela clutched the metal box in her lap, her gray hair hanging straight and dull. Yolanda took a swig of water and handed the bottle over to Sonja. Suddenly, a thought occurred to her. Welo had a long silver scar on his hand, the length of his palm. She used to trace it with her fingers as a child. "What was Welo's first name?" she asked. Yolanda had only ever called him Welo, but something about Wela's stories rang familiar to her.

"Benjamín." Wela's eyes darted to the ground.

The news shook Yolanda as she stared at Wela, incredulous at this revelation. "Welo is Benjamín? From your story?" Yolanda shook her head in disbelief.

"You married your sister's fiancé?" Sonja asked, her mouth hanging wide.

"Well, yes. But you see, it was many years later and she had been long gone by then," Wela said quickly.

Forty-two

LONG GONE. We were both devastated by her death for many years and wrote back and forth about our lives, unable to find anyone else who understood what we had lost. We clung to each other, forever bonded by her tragedy.

I saw him again when I went to college. He was a professor and I was a student. He had never dated anyone after Violeta. We started to spend time together discussing science, the butterflies, and different types of research I could do with them to hide the truth about myself.

I didn't plan it.

Sometimes things just happen.

He was someone who understood my skill and someone I

could trust. I didn't have to hide it from him. He understood how I could use it and apply it to science, which is all I ever wanted. I loved science, but I had to figure out how to incorporate the butterflies into my career. If I wanted a semblance of a normal life, I had to draw attention away from myself and the skill.

But Benjamín wouldn't give it up. He was as determined as ever to figure out how to explain the trait. He wanted me to live a normal life too. The difference was the tragedy with my sister made him stop chasing the rumors of witchcraft.

Once we had Alejandra, I asked him to stop studying the trait once and for all, but he couldn't let it go. It was like having a daughter made his obsession worse. He asked me questions about Mami's family, her sisters, her mother. At first I would answer him and tell him what I knew, but after a while I grew tired and ignored his questions.

It was exhausting, I didn't want to keep fighting with him, but when Raúl left me the house and the orchard, of course he wanted to learn everything he could.

Like clockwork, that spring, the tree—her tree—bloomed. And in fall we made our way to the tree and stood between the graves of my family to harvest the nuts.

Generations of the Rodríguez family were buried under the tree, their old, crumbling gravestones worn from the years in the harsh desert.

"So your entire family buried here was a Rodríguez?" Benjamín asked. "With the family trait?"

"Most of them had the trait," I said. "Not Papá."

Benjamín stood over Violeta's grave. "She's still down there." He dug his palms into his temples. I didn't know what he was about to do.

The next day Benjamín took a shovel out to the tree and dug until he reached her.

When he brought her bones to the lab, I screamed. "How could you? You loved her! She was my sister!"

He couldn't look at me for a long time. I think he was ashamed of what he'd done. I didn't speak a word to him for months, and he eventually moved himself into the old casita.

He scraped her bones, studied her cells, and performed test after test on them. He carved Punnett squares all over the inside of the old casita like a madman.

But he never did figure it out.

When he took her bones, the orchard died.

The drought came. The river dried up, the ditches emptied, and the few pecan trees that had started to come back, shriveled and died.

After he took her bones, the tree never bloomed again.

It's not beautiful anymore. It's eerie, the way it stands on the butte, its naked limbs twisting in every direction.

The town blamed me.

Everyone said it was me who cursed this place. They said it was me who caused the drought. But it wasn't me.

It was him.

It was many years before I could even speak to Benjamín again.

Instead, I busied myself with raising your mamá and my own research—the butterflies.

One day, many years later, he presented me with a box. This box. He begged me to forgive him and take him back. He said he'd only wanted to help me and our daughter have a normal life. He told me he was sorry for what he had done and he'd had her cremated properly. He was going to bring her back to the tree and bury her.

It was a nice thought, but he never did.

I know because the pecan tree never bloomed again.

That's what's in this box.

Violeta's ashes.

And we are bringing her back to where she belongs.

Forty-three

WELA'S eyes closed and the sisters were alone again, pulling the serape and trudging up the rocky terrain. The sky turned gray as the dark clouds rolled in. Thunder rumbled in the distance.

"I can't believe Welo was Benjamín." Sonja checked to make sure Wela was asleep.

"I guess I'm not surprised." Yolanda held a corner of the serape and carefully picked her way across the trail. A few sunbeams radiated through the dark clouds, casting rays onto the rolling mountains way out in the distance. "They have a lot in common if you think about it. Science. They both lost someone very important to them."

"But still, he was engaged to her sister."

"I can't believe he dug up her bones." Yolanda shuddered. "I thought he loved her." The revelations about Welo were shaking her to her core. She had a hard time imagining Welo doing such a horrible thing. He'd always had ambition, but she'd never seen him do anything that could be considered so wrong.

"Welo was always more interested in science than anything else. He spent hours in that workshop, filling notebooks."

"I know, but I see him so differently now—knowing all of this." Yolanda couldn't accept the new knowledge and understanding of a man she had admired so much. It was unsettling. Had she been blinded by her love for him? She thought of how she had spent all of those hours in the library, desperate to find a cure to save Welo. They were so much alike, chasing scientific answers at any cost. Was it possible for him to be both a wonderful and loving *abuelo* and also a man who'd done some terrible things in his past? She thought back to when he was dying and had asked her to finish his work. He'd still wanted an answer. He had never given it up. Maybe that was why he never took Violeta's ashes back to the tree. Yolanda shuddered again. She didn't want to end up that way.

They climbed the trail, picking their way over boulders and rocks, carefully guiding Wela on the serape up and over the terrain. The pecan tree was getting closer. Sonja was agile climbing over the rocks and knew exactly where to grab to pull herself up. Yolanda slipped, skittering rocks down the mountainside.

They were about halfway up the trail, taking a rest, when the butterflies began to leave.

They landed briefly on Wela's forehead, as if saying goodbye, and then one by one, drifted away as the blanket slowly lowered toward to the ground.

Sonja desperately waved her arms. "No!" she cried. She shut her eyes, concentrating, determined to keep the butterflies close, but her skill wasn't developed enough. The bees couldn't hold the weight of Wela alone, and before long they flew out from the serape and Wela was on the ground.

Wela woke and tried to summon her butterflies back, but she was too weak. She could barely raise her frail arms from the ground.

They had made it so far and were getting so close, but now everything was gone.

"Why would they leave?" Sonja touched a wildflower on the serape.

"I'm growing weaker, *mija*," Wela said. "And they know it."

"But how will we get you to the tree? We're running out of time." Yolanda gazed up the rocky trail toward the pecan tree.

Wela sat back on her elbows and placed the box next to her on the ground. "I think Yolanda can help."

"Me?" Yolanda stepped back. "What am I supposed to do?"

"I think you know," Wela said.

Yolanda swallowed hard. "So it's true, then? I have one?"

"Have one what?" Sonja rested her hands on her hips, a small swarm of the bees buzzing noisily around her head.

"Yours came later, probably masked by your sadness," Wela said. "The same thing happened with Raúl."

"Raúl?" Yolanda knelt in the dirt next to Wela. "But he didn't have a skill."

"Oh, but he did."

Forty-four

RAÚL'S skill eventually did come, though the sorrow we all felt hid it for a long, long time. But once he was a little older and after our parents were gone, he figured it out.

One day he met a girl in town. And she was a happy, delightful soul. It was the first time in a long time he felt happy too. Truly happy. And it was for no reason at all.

Raúl was an empath. He could feel other people's emotions. If they were nearby, he felt it. In his soul, in his heart, in his mind. From his head to his heart to his toes. It was amazing, but also difficult for him.

Imagine carrying all the weight of the world's emotions right inside your heart.

All the time.

That's why the war was so hard on him. He took on all the death, the sorrow, and the fear.

And he couldn't change it. He couldn't do anything to ease the pain of others or himself. He just felt it.

Before Violeta's death, Raúl was a quiet, soft soul. He did as he was told and never caused too much trouble. But after Violeta, and after his skill came, he took the feelings of our family—the sorrow, the grief, and the intense sadness—into himself.

It was too much for him in the end. He felt too much too often and couldn't escape it ever. I felt sorry for him. It must have been so hard to live like that, with those emotions inside of him all the time. We were all sad. We were all grieving. But we didn't have to physically feel everyone else's sadness too.

I'm not sure why I never told Benjamín about Raúl's gift. Maybe I thought he would try to dig him up too or exploit him in some way. I believe Benjamín loved us, but I also believe his ambition was something he could not control.

I think if things were different, maybe Mami would have been able to help Raúl cope with his gift.

But in the end he was on his own.

We were all on our own.

forty-five

"So, why is my skill here now?" Yolanda sat back on her heels. "Why all of a sudden did it show up on this journey through the desert?"

"Because sometimes it takes time." Wela placed her hand on Yolanda's arm. "It's true, every person in our family has the skill. And every person's skill came around age twelve, but it's not perfect. Some realized their skills a little earlier, some a little later. Mami told me my *tía* Valentina was reading minds a lot earlier than she let on."

"I don't know—"

Wela grasped Yolanda's hand gently. Her eyes were warm and pleading. "It won't hurt to try."

What if it didn't work? What if she didn't really have a skill at all? Then she thought of Mamá giving up her own life for Yolanda to live hers. She rose onto her knees and spread her trembling hands out, hovering them over Wela. If Mamá could do it, so could she.

"Deep breaths," Wela said. It was the same thing she told Sonja when they worked with the bees.

Yolanda closed her eyes and took a deep breath in, her shoulders rising, and then let it out in one big rush. What if she couldn't help Wela? The possibility of failure washed over her. They had come this far. She couldn't give up now. She had to try.

She steadied her hands and opened her eyes. She took a breath in, pursed her lips, and blew the cool air over Wela's body, starting at her head and moving down to her waist. The warmth inside her lungs changed to a cool healing breath as it moved from her lips and over Wela's body. She took another breath and started at Wela's waist, blowing the healing air down to her feet. Goose bumps rose on Wela's wrinkled brown arms. Yolanda repeated this over and over again until she grew light-headed. She sat back on her heels.

When she looked at Wela again, her hair was curlier and a bit whiter.

Wela lifted her arms and Sonja helped her sit up.

Yolanda slipped the *chanclas* on Wela's feet. Groaning and unsteady, Wela slowly rose as her legs shook underneath her.

"You can heal." Sonja's eyes shone with pride.

Yolanda's heart swelled. She had done it. It was an incredible feeling, knowing that she had made Wela better. A huge weight had been lifted from her shoulders.

Wela steadied herself, placed her arms on Yolanda's shoulders, and looked her in the eyes.

"You did it," Wela said, her chin quivering. "You have it now."

"I'm so happy I made you better!" Yolanda threw her arms around Wela excitedly. "Now everything will be okay."

"Oh, *mija*! You healed me—you did, but only for a little while. I still need to get to the pecan tree."

Yolanda pulled back. "But why? You look so much better."

"I feel better. But this isn't a cure." Wela looked Yolanda in the eyes. "If your mamá taught me anything, it was that you can't heal everything. Some processes naturally take over."

Yolanda's eyes widened as she thought of Hasik. "Hasik. Will he be okay?"

"I think so, *mija*." Wela patted her on the back. "You

got to him pretty quickly." Wela cleared her throat. "*Mijas*, give me a moment. I'd like a moment to clear my head."

The girls made sure Wela was safe, sitting on a rock, and walked a ways up the path.

"What will happen to us if Dad doesn't make it home?" Sonja asked, running her fingers through stalks of wheat-colored grass. It began to turn green. "That social worker will be there when we get back."

Yolanda sat down on a rock and stretched her legs in front of her. "Wela will still be here."

Sonja scoffed. "You don't believe that, do you? You can't possibly think the pecan tree is going to save her life. You are smarter than that."

Yolanda recoiled. "Of course it's going to save her life. Why else would we be doing this?"

"Yolanda, she's dying."

"But the pecan tree. She said everything will be set right when we get to the pecan tree." Sonja's words swam in her head. Sonja was wrong. She had to be. Wela had said *no mentiras*. She said everything would be set right.

Sonja shook her head. "You heard what she said. Some processes can't be healed. It won't make any difference."

It wasn't true. The pecan tree would save her. It had to.

⇒⊱

When they looked back at Wela, she was asleep. Yolanda ran over and gently shook her awake. Wela stirred and, with Yolanda's help, stood on shaky legs. Sonja picked up the metal box and sidled up to Wela's other side, and they began climbing up the trail.

Yolanda glanced at Wela's curls. She was fine. She looked so much better now. She tried to push Sonja's words from her mind.

"Something is bothering me," Yolanda said. "If Welo was so obsessed with figuring out the trait, why didn't he ever study Mamá?"

Wela laughed. "Because if he had, I would have killed him. And when your Mamá's skill came when she was twelve, I made her promise me she wouldn't become his lab rat. You and your mamá are similar in that way. No one is going to make you do anything you don't want to." Wela brushed Yolanda's cheek. "You remind me so much of her—beautiful . . . smart . . . fiery."

Yolanda felt warm thinking about being like Mamá, such a strong woman who sacrificed her life for her daughters. She was happy she shared the family skill with her, even if it was also scary.

Sonja looked toward the pecan tree. It stood tall, a bare black spindly tree up on a hill. The hot afternoon sun was beginning to dip lower and lower in the sky. Dark black clouds moved quickly toward them, and the wind was picking up.

"We've got to move a lot faster," Sonja said, swatting a bee from her forehead.

Forty-six

SONJA dropped the last of their water on Wela's parched lips. "Wela, are you okay?" Sonja asked.

Her eyelids fluttered. "I'm so tired, *mijas*."

Yolanda held Wela up, her weight bearing down on her. She was exhausted and her curls were gone. Her hair was straight and gray again. Yolanda looked up the trail. The pecan tree swayed in the wind, its branches contorting against the darkening sky. "We don't have much farther to go. Do you think you can make it?'

"I'm so tired." Wela's pale fingers clutched the handle of the metal box, and her knees buckled.

Yolanda crouched next to Wela, closed her eyes, and

breathed the cool healing breath over her body. *Please, please, please work*, she thought. When she opened her eyes, Wela didn't look any better. Her hair remained gray and straight, her eyes sunken and dark.

It hadn't worked this time.

A lump formed in Yolanda's throat. Wela's words, *some processes naturally take over the body*, rang in Yolanda's mind even though she tried to push them out.

Wela looked only slightly better after a few minutes of rest. The girls helped her stand, but her legs trembled underneath her. Sonja and Yolanda exchanged a worried glance. They each took an arm and helped Wela start the climb.

The conversation with Sonja was bothering Yolanda.

"What's the pecan tree supposed to do when we get there? How will it heal you?" Yolanda felt her voice shake. In her mind she knew it wasn't possible to beat death, but she was so sure when Wela said everything would be set right, it meant she would be healed. That everything would go back to the way it was. That everything would be okay.

She had to know now.

"*Mija*." Wela lowered her eyes. "It is not what you think." Wela turned to her.

Yolanda's stomach dropped and she let go of Wela's arm. She felt herself say, "So, what is it then?" But in her mind she was screaming, *Don't say it!*

It couldn't be true.

Wela took both of Yolanda's hands and looked in her eyes. "The point of life is . . . eventually we will die. That is what makes this life so beautiful. The fact that it is finite. The fact that we do not exist forever. That is what makes life a gift."

Tears filled Yolanda's eyes. This couldn't be happening. Not again. Not to Wela. "But if I could save you, we would have more time together. You could be here for when Sonja and I do great things with our lives. You raised us. Don't you want to see what happens to us?"

"Oh, *mija*," Wela said, bringing Yolanda in a close embrace. "Of course I would love to see you grow up. I know you both will do amazing things. But we don't get to pick when we go. And believe me, no matter how old or young you are, it will always feel much too soon."

Yolanda clung to Wela and played with her hair. It used to be so curly and white, so full of life. "I don't want to lose you." Wela had taught her so much. She had been her mamá, her *abuela*, and at times her dad, too. What would happen to their lives without her? The familiar tightness hooked in her chest, and she pulled away. "But if we didn't have to die, then we wouldn't feel such pain. Imagine your life if you had never lost Violeta or Mamá. Wouldn't life have been so much better?"

Wela's tired eyes grew sad and dark. "I would have loved to spend more time with them. Any more time would have been a great gift. Losing them was extremely painful, but we don't get to pick what happens in this life. We just . . . don't."

"We wouldn't know happiness either," Sonja offered, her eyes shining with tears. "If we never experienced sadness and loss, life wouldn't be as colorful."

"Exactly," Wela said.

The new understanding of the journey rocked Yolanda, making her dizzy.

This was a death journey.

"So, this entire trip—through the desert—is not to save your life? You lied to me!" Yolanda let go of Wela and ran her palms through her wild hair. "I thought the pecan tree was going to heal you—make you better!" Hot, angry tears poured down her cheeks, and her chest felt like it was going to explode. How would they possibly go on without her? "How could you? *No mentiras!* Remember?"

Wela's cracked lips turned into a solemn frown, and she held her arms out for Yolanda. But Yolanda turned and ran. There was a rumble of thunder in the distance as she ran down the mountain, rocks sliding underneath her feet. The wind whipped her hair. She ran so fast, she almost lost her footing.

"Yo!" Sonja called. "Come back! We can't lose you."

Forty-seven

YOLANDA couldn't lose Wela. Not like Welo. Not again. This was not going to happen to her.

Yolanda bolted down the mountain, her heart pounding, tears blurring her vision.

She couldn't take Wela to the pecan tree. For what? To let her die? It was too much to bear.

She was moving so fast, her body lurched over her feet. She tried to slow herself, but it was too late.

She hit the ground with a *thud* and plunged down the mountainside, toppling head over feet. Dust and dirt scattered around her as she desperately grasped for anything to slow her descent.

A sharp rock tore through her thigh as she slid farther and farther down the mountain.

Crack!

Her left foot twisted underneath her, sending a shock of pain through her body.

When she finally reached the bottom, she slowed, flopped onto her back, and looked up at the dark sky, breathing heavily. Her heart pounded in her throat.

Pinching her eyes shut, she lay there and moaned, waiting for the pain in her ankle to pass. When she finally got the courage to move her foot, a white-hot pain shot through her body, stealing her breath.

A low rumble of thunder echoed in the distance, and Yolanda opened her eyes. Dark clouds billowed overhead, and the wind picked up, blowing cool air over her.

She propped herself up on her elbows and looked at her leg. She had a bleeding gash in her thigh, and her ankle was already starting to swell.

She tried to move her foot again.

The pain seared through her, stealing her breath again and forcing her to lie back.

How could Wela do this to her? If it wasn't to save her life, then what was this journey for? Why would Wela make her come all this way if there was no hope to save her? Had she been lying to her this entire time? First Welo and now Wela? She couldn't face losing her, too.

Her heart ached as much as her leg.

Then she heard a distant jingling.

Rosalind Franklin popped through the brush. She ran to Yolanda and licked her face.

"Hey, girl." Yolanda pet her ears. Then the tears came. "I'm so happy to see you." And she was. Her dog had a way of making her feel better when she felt her worst. Rosalind Franklin wagged her stubby tail, wiggling her entire body. She sniffed Yolanda's ankle and licked it once before placing her paws on Yolanda's chest and laying her head down. Yolanda hugged her tight.

After a few minutes, Ghita and Hasik arrived. Hasik was hobbling and slouched over a walking stick, while Ghita held him up on the other side. His lips had returned to their normal color, and he looked much better. He smiled as soon as he saw her, and Yolanda's stomach did a flip-flop.

"Hasik!" A wave of relief washed over her, giving her a break from the pain. "What are you doing here?" She was relieved to see them both, but mostly Hasik. The only person who seemed to understand her.

Ghita helped Hasik hobble his way up to Yolanda.

"Look," he said, stretching his foot out. "I'm doing much better. We saw the butterflies leave. They flew right over us. We thought you might need help. I'm just really slow." Hasik looked down at Yolanda lying on the ground. "Are you okay?"

"What happened?" Ghita glanced at Yolanda's swollen ankle and then averted her eyes. She was always a bit squeamish.

"I'm not going." Yolanda shook her head and crossed her arms. "I'm not taking Wela to the tree."

Hasik sat on the ground next to her and threw his walking stick down.

Her eyes locked with his.

"I can't save her," Yolanda said, her voice catching. The tears brimmed in her eyes, and she turned away.

"You didn't really think you could?" Hasik said softly. He rubbed her shoulder. "Not really."

Yolanda nodded furiously. "But I did. She told me the tree would save her life." Yolanda's shoulders fell back as she thought it over again. "Not exactly in those words, but something like that. She said everything would be set right when we got to the tree." She pressed her lips together and swallowed the lump in her throat. She really had believed it, even though somewhere inside her she knew it wasn't possible. She wanted so badly for it to be true. "She let me believe the tree would save her life."

Hasik wrapped his large arms around her in a warm, tight hug and whispered in her ear, "You will regret it." He pulled away and looked her straight in the eyes. "If you miss this, you will regret it."

As Yolanda looked back into Hasik's kind brown eyes, something inside her shifted. She thought about the story he'd told her about Nani and being too afraid to help his mother. She thought about her own regret in avoiding the truth about Welo and all the time she'd missed with him, trying so desperately to avoid the inevitable. Hasik was right. She couldn't do that to Wela. She couldn't do that to herself, either. If Sonja took Wela to the tree by herself, Yolanda would regret it for the rest of her life. Just as she did with Welo.

Those last moments she missed.

Everything . . . she missed.

She felt a hand on her shoulder.

Ghita.

"I'm sorry." Ghita squeezed her shoulder. "I'm so sorry."

"But she's going to die," Yolanda said, the tears dripping down her nose.

"But you can help her. You can help her get where she needs to go." Ghita stooped down and grabbed her hand. "The way she wants to go."

Yolanda let Ghita hold her hand. It was comforting to have Ghita there.

"When my Nani died, I was so scared. But my mother

told me death is a part of life and it was our duty to help her. And so I did. And even though it hurt so bad, the worst hurt I've ever felt, I don't regret any of it. I don't regret being there for her final moments. I don't regret helping my mother bathe her. I don't regret helping wrap her up in white cloth and putting her on the pyre. I thought I was going to faint, I was so scared, but I don't wish it was different. It just was. In fact, now, looking back, I feel honored to have been part of it."

Yolanda looked at Ghita. Even if they were no longer going to be best friends, it was time to let things go between them. It was time to apologize.

"I'm so sorry I wasn't there for you," Yolanda said, gripping Ghita's hands between hers. Her voice shook. "I'm sorry I made it all about me."

Ghita's chin quivered, and she squeezed Yolanda's hands back. "I'm sorry too. For all of it."

Thunder rumbled in the distance. Yolanda looked to Hasik. "I'm going to need your help. Hold my foot straight."

Hasik's eyes widened. "Won't it hurt to move it?"

Yolanda nodded. "Yep, but I think it's only sprained. I think I can fix it."

Hasik hobbled down by her foot and crouched down. "Okay, here I go."

Yolanda sucked in a deep breath and held it. When he

straightened her foot, the pain in her ankle shot up her leg.

She sucked in a breath, lay back to catch her breath, and then sat up.

"Watch," she said, grasping her thigh between her hands. She took a deep breath in and out, blowing the air over the gash in her thigh first. The trickle of blood began to disappear into the wound. Fresh pink tissue began to knit the wound closed. Then she bent her knee, bringing her foot in close. She pursed her lips and breathed the cool healing air over her ankle. The coolness spread under her palms, and the pain began to disappear.

Hasik glanced from his ankle to her leg. And back again.

"Hey—did you—?"

"Cool, huh?" she said. "Like Violeta—and just like Mamá." She took another deep breath and blew the cool air over her ankle again. The swelling began to disappear. After a few minutes, she wiggled her foot. There was still a distant ache, but it was better.

Ghita and Hasik helped her climb to her feet. She scrunched up her face in anticipation as she shifted her weight onto her left leg.

Her ankle held.

She gazed down the trail, across the riverbed, and over the tall, tall grass to where the house was supposed to be. To where she really wanted to go.

Home.

But this time would be different. This time she would have to do exactly what she didn't want to.

She turned away from her friends and looked up the rocky trail toward the pecan tree. Its looming bare-boned black skeleton stood tall. The dark clouds were gaining ground quickly. Lightning struck across the sky in a white flash, and a large crack of thunder followed.

Hasik handed her his walking stick, and she started up the mountain.

Her ankle ached, but it held as she used the walking stick to help her shift her weight and climb the trail. Gusts of wind whipped her hair, and another crack of thunder rumbled in the distance.

She couldn't leave Sonja to do this alone.

The cool drops stung her cheeks, mixing her tears with the rain. With each step up the trail, she wanted to turn and run, but she forced herself to keep going up. One step at time. One foot in front of the other. *You can do this*, she thought. As her feet began to slide on the rocks, she abandoned the walking stick and got down on all fours. She clawed her way up the trail, reaching the spot where she had left them.

But they were gone.

Forty-eight

YOLANDA'S heart sank. What if she lost them? What if it was already too late? She stumbled up the path, balancing on the boulders, her feet slipping in the mud. The pecan tree stood menacing, its dark limbs twisting and shaking in the wind.

Then she spotted them. Wela leaned on Sonja as they hobbled slowly up the trail. They were so close.

"Sonja!" she called. But the wind carried her voice away.

Yolanda broke into a half run, but her weakened ankle wobbled and she fell, her knee slamming into the ground. She got up and kept running, the blood dripping in a warm stream down her leg.

Just a little farther and she would reach them. They were only a few hundred feet away. Yolanda glanced to her left at the steep drop off the side of the mountain.

Then her hair stood on end, tickling the back of her neck. A shiver ran up her spine.

Crack! BOOM!

The sky brightened white as lightning struck the pecan tree. The thunder that followed shook her chest and rang in her ears. She froze, unable to think.

Then she threw herself on the ground.

When she looked up, the pecan tree splintered down the middle with a loud *crack*.

"No!" Yolanda screamed. "Wela! Sonja!"

When they turned, a look of relief swept over Sonja's sunburned cheeks. They waited for her to catch up as the rain pelted them. Sonja was breathing hard, holding Wela up by herself. Wela's soaked hair hung down her back as she gripped the box.

"I knew you would come back." The rain ran in the deep creases of Wela's face as she squeezed Yolanda's arm.

"If this is not going to save your life," Yolanda said, "then why are we going to this tree?" She knew in her heart something would be set right. While Wela had a lot of secrets, she always meant it when she said *no mentiras*.

"I have a theory." Wela patted the wet metal box against

her thigh. "Or maybe it's a hope. But as Mami used to say, it's a strange land."

"I'm so glad you came back, Yo." Sonja gave her a tired smile.

Yolanda supported Wela's weight. The rain began to fall harder, stinging her with freezing drops. The lump in her throat grew. These were going to be her last moments with Wela. She had to make them count.

Crack! BOOM!

As they picked their way up to the face of the last ridge, thunder rumbled all around them. They climbed together, a sister under each of Wela's arms, and helped her reach the base of the ridge.

With every step, the tightness in Yolanda's chest squeezed so hard, she could hardly breathe. She was getting closer and closer to saying goodbye.

Yolanda let go of Wela and climbed the slippery face of the mountain, her hands clawing and slipping in the orange mud. When she reached the top, Wela handed her the metal box. She took it and then pulled Wela up and over as Sonja pushed, her feet skidding on the rocks, causing the boulders to tumble down the mountainside into the ravine below.

Yolanda held out a hand to help Sonja over the edge. Her hand was wet and slippery, and as Sonja gripped it she tried to pull herself up, but she was weak. She scrambled to find a foothold, slipping in the mud.

"You take her," Sonja said, breathless, her lips pale. "Take Wela. I'm too tired."

"No." Yolanda gripped Sonja's hands even harder. "I'm not leaving you behind."

The wind whipped at Sonja's red braids, and Yolanda mustered her last bit of strength. With all her might she pulled hard, and Sonja came over the ridge.

As they both fell into an exhausted heap next to Wela, the wind and the rain stopped, leaving an eerie calm behind. Everything was quiet.

Yolanda propped herself up and looked around. Fifty feet away was the base of the tree. Splintered bark twisted up from the ground, the scent of scorched wood burning in her nostrils. Crumbling gravestones marked the area around the tree.

Wela's eyes were closed, but her fingers were wrapped tightly around the metal box. "Wela," Yolanda said.

Wela's eyes popped open.

Sonja climbed to her feet, unsteady.

"Come on," Yolanda said, reaching for her sister.

A vacant look crossed Sonja's face.

The boulders Sonja was standing on began to rumble. A large crack formed between the sisters, and Sonja's eyes widened as the boulders tumbled down the ridge.

"No!" Yolanda screamed, and ran for the edge. She spotted Sonja lying across a pair of large boulders, her freckled cheek bloodied. "I'm stuck." Sonja moaned. Her left arm was wedged between the two boulders.

"Try to move it." Yolanda skidded down the muddy face of the mountain.

Sonja screamed. "I can't!"

With the break in the rain, the bees had returned and were orbiting Sonja.

Yolanda tried to avoid them, but they were multiplying. "You have to move the bees."

Sonja moaned, her eyelids fluttering.

Yolanda wiggled herself between the two boulders, bracing herself, hoping they wouldn't give with all the rain and slam down the mountain.

The bees seemed angry as they swarmed Sonja's lolling head. Yolanda grabbed Sonja's free arm and pulled hard, moving her body slightly from the boulder. She reached down and tried to pull Sonja's other arm from the crevice.

Sonja screamed.

It was stuck tight.

Then Yolanda felt a sting on her hand.

And then another on her cheek.

And another.

Come on, Sonja. Come on.

Finally Sonja's arm broke free, and Yolanda dragged her over to the slippery face of the ridge, feeling the painful stings all over her hands and face. Sonja clawed her way up the ledge, Yolanda pushing her from behind. The stings kept coming, and Yolanda's vision began to blur. Sonja's hand appeared, and she pulled Yolanda over the ledge.

When Yolanda reached the top, she fell back and quickly blew cool air over her arm and hand. She blew air from her lower lip over her face, and as the rain began to fall again, her eyes closed.

"Goodbye, Wela," she whispered.

Forty-nine

"YOLANDA ... Yolanda."

Yolanda groaned and rolled over. Someone was shaking her awake. When she opened her eyes, the gray sky spun all around. "What happened?"

"I'm so sorry!" Sonja winced as she moved her arm. "The bees! They stung you. I'm so sorry."

Yolanda felt the swollen pink lumps covering her arms and face. "How am I not . . . dead?" Yolanda sat up. She didn't have her medicine with her. She scratched at an itchy lump on her cheek.

"I think you healed yourself." A pair of bees flew around Sonja's messy braids.

"How's your arm?"

"Sore." Sonja examined her arm, bloodied and scraped. "But not broken."

"Good." Yolanda climbed to her feet, swaying from dizziness. She glanced at Wela, propped next to a boulder, her eyes closed, her head slumped to the side. Her chest was barely rising with each breath.

This was it.

"We have to go."

Sonja and Yolanda picked up Wela, who stirred softly. Yolanda ducked under her arm and lifted her up. They stumbled the last fifty feet to the pecan tree and sat Wela at the base of it. Her head lolled to the side. She was barely conscious.

The tree was much bigger up close than Yolanda had imagined it would be. The lightning had struck the tree right in the center, splitting it down the middle of its massive trunk. Shards of splintered bark radiated from the center.

Dread filled the pit of her stomach. This was the moment she had hoped would never have to happen.

But it was time.

Raindrops dripping from the branches sizzled and steamed as they pelted the singed bark. The area around the tree was littered with gravestones of different sizes, square and rounded, each one adorned with a different Rodríguez name. Yolanda walked around the tree and looked at them.

The tightness in her throat made it hard to swallow. She gulped as she imagined a gravestone like the others with Wela's name on it.

Sonja choked on her tears, her face breaking into a grimace. "She can't go, Yo. Not yet." Sonja buried her face in her hands. "I'm not ready." She looked up at Yolanda, her eyes watery and red. Her bottom lip trembled.

"I'm not ready, either." Yolanda's voice quivered. But she had to be strong for Sonja. Like Sonja had been for her. "Wela needs to go the way she wants, with us by her side."

Tears streamed down Sonja's freckled, sunburned cheeks as she shook her head in disbelief. "I can't bear to lose her."

"Neither can I," Yolanda said. The ache in her chest hurt so bad she couldn't breathe.

Fifty

YOLANDA walked between the graves and read a name out loud.

"Santiago Rodríguez."

"*Creador de fuego*," Wela replied sleepily.

"*Fuego*," Sonja said. "Something to do with fire."

"He was a fire maker. My *tío*."

"Valentina Rodríguez-Domínguez." Yolanda walked by another grave.

"*Telepatía*," Wela replied.

"Telepathy?" Yolanda asked.

Wela nodded. "A *tía*—Mami's sister. You couldn't get away with anything with her." Wela laughed weakly.

"She always knew when you were lying."

"Carmen Rodríguez."

"Mami," Wela said softly. "*Clarividente.* Clairvoyant."

"Valeria Rodríguez-López."

"Ah, *mi bisabuela.* My great-grandmother. *Las abejas y las plantas.* She worked with bees and plants—like Sonja." Wela smiled and held out a hand. Sonja grasped it and squeezed it. She sniffed hard.

Yolanda bent down and stuck a finger in the grooves of one of the gravestones. Alejandra Rodríguez-O'Connell. *Curandera.*

Mamá. Healer.

A heaviness filled her chest. *I hope I make you proud, Mamá.*

"Did you find Violeta's?" Wela craned her neck. "It should be right next to Mami's."

Yolanda looked next to Mami's gravestone. There were two. One smaller and unmarked and a larger one. Violeta Rodríguez. *Curandera.*

"Here it is." She knelt in front of it.

Yolanda and Sonja got down on their knees and dug, with their hands, a deep hole at the base of Violeta's gravestone.

"*Mija,* hand me a rock." Wela held out her hand. Sonja handed her a heavy rock, and Wela hit the lock of the box over and over again, the metal clinking, until it finally broke open.

The box was filled with dusty gray ashes.

Wela carefully dumped the contents of the box into the hole and covered it up with dirt. "Forgive me, Violeta, for all the wrong I ever caused you."

"I don't want to do this," Yolanda said, her heart twisting with dread. "Not yet."

Sonja shook her head. "Me either."

Yolanda looked at her sister. "We'll get through it together." She reached for Sonja's hand. Sonja bit her lip, squeezed Yolanda's hand, and nodded.

They helped Wela lie down next to her sister's grave.

"Take these." Wela slipped the *chanclas* off her feet and handed them to Yolanda. "And take them back. You can give them to that dog of yours." Wela smiled.

Yolanda clutched Wela's shoes and sat next to her. The girls covered Wela with the serape, tucking it underneath her chin. Wela reached out with both hands.

One for each girl.

Wela's eyelids fluttered.

Yolanda picked a leaf out of Wela's hair. She looked so different without her butterflies, as though a part of her was missing. Tears brimmed in Yolanda's eyes, her heart heavy. This was it.

The air chilled, misty and cool.

"*Aye, mijas*, this is my goodbye to you. I have enjoyed this life so much." Wela turned to Sonja.

"Sonja, you need to have confidence. No one is truer than you. You can handle those bees. You can handle anything." Wela closed her eyes. She gave Sonja a single nod. "You are enough." Yolanda could see Sonja's lip trembling, and it made her want to look away, but she didn't.

Sonja was in as much pain as she was.

"Yolanda, like Raúl," Wela said, "you may struggle with your skill, *mija*. I always knew it would come, but you will only realize your potential when you learn to let things go. *Sé libre, mi niña curiosa.* Be free, my curious girl."

Wela continued. "Love each other. One of the greatest gifts in this life is having a sister. Believe me. Take care of each other. Now it is my turn to be with my sister."

Yolanda grabbed her sister's hand and held it tight. Sonja gave her a grateful smile. As painful as this was, at least they weren't alone. They were doing it together.

Yolanda had one last question. "Why the tree, Wela? Why here?"

"You'll see." Wela smiled. Then she let go of their hands and tucked her arms underneath the serape. Her chest moved up and down a few more times before it finally stopped. Sonja and Yolanda stood together, heads bent as the raindrops fell all around them.

A curling mist crept in and settled underneath the pecan tree, shielding their view of Wela. When it passed through, she was gone, leaving only the serape in her place.

Yolanda's heart split in half as she grabbed Sonja and hugged her tight. She was the only other person in the world who understood exactly how Yolanda was feeling in that moment, and she was so grateful they were together.

Their tears hit the ground with force. The rain mixed with their tears, starting with a puddle between their feet, running down the rocky hill and into the earth. Yolanda's heart was heavy, but she knew she had done the right thing. This was what Wela wanted, to be with her sister again. Sonja's entire body heaved, and Yolanda held her tight.

When Yolanda looked back, the rain and mud had buried the serape, leaving only a small corner visible.

Yolanda rested her head on Sonja's shoulder, and they wept together.

Fifty-one

THE RAIN slowed and then stopped as the bright sun warmed Yolanda's shoulders. Raindrops sparkled on the burnt black branches of the pecan tree.

"Hold on a second." Yolanda wiped her tears and went to her backpack, dug inside, and pulled out the compass.

"Mamá's compass!" Sonja cried, grabbing it from Yolanda. "I was looking for this."

"I know. I'm sorry. I took it." Yolanda hung her head. "I think I broke it. It keeps spinning. . . ."

"No, it works. It's pointing north." Sonja turned and faced north—toward home. The cloudy mist was moving fast, curling away and dissolving in the heat.

"The house!" Sonja jumped up. "It's back!"

The tall grass had shrunk back to a few inches, and they could see the white wraparound porch way out in the distance. Rays of sunlight shone through the clouds, radiating on the valley of the mountains.

Yolanda smiled and then turned back to the pecan tree. "What's that?" She stepped closer.

The split trunk and its dead branches were covered in orange blossoms, which were vibrating and humming.

"I didn't know pecan trees had orange flowers," Yolanda said.

From the center of the split trunk, a thin green sapling had emerged. On a fragile branch was a single white flower. Sonja stepped closer. "They don't," she said. "They're white."

Yolanda moved toward the tree and realized the orange flowers weren't flowers at all. "Those aren't flowers. Those are—"

"Butterflies," Sonja said.

At that moment the butterflies all left the tree at once. Thousands of them pumped their wings and flew all around them. Yolanda held out her arms and laughed through her tears.

Wela.

One landed on her index finger. It flapped its wings a few times before flying off into the whirl. Slowly, the butterflies trickled away, toward home, until there were none left at all.

Yolanda looked back toward the house and shielded her eyes from the bright sun.

"Well, it's time to go."

As they hiked down the trail, Yolanda was sad, but she was also relieved.

It was over.

Sonja's bees flew around her disheveled braids. Now she didn't have to worry about being around Sonja and her bees anymore.

Yolanda reached out for Sonja's hand. Sonja let Yolanda grab it for a moment before turning back down the hill.

"Wow." Sonja pointed. "Look at that."

The river was rushing and flowing again, filled to the brim with cool, clear water. Hasik, Ghita, and Rosalind Franklin shouldn't be far.

"What's going to happen to us?" Sonja asked as they picked their way carefully down the muddy trail.

"It doesn't matter where we end up," Yolanda said, gazing back at the pecan tree. "As long as we're together."

Fifty-two

WHEN they reached the others, Sonja immediately ran to Ghita. Ghita patted her back over and over again and let her cry in her arms. "It's going to be okay. It's okay."

Hasik was holding Rosalind Franklin, who wiggled frantically.

"Hey, girl." Yolanda took her out of Hasik's arms as Rosalind Franklin sniffed and licked all over her salt-crusted cheeks. She handed her one of Wela's *chanclas* and set her on the ground. Rosalind Franklin pranced happily away with the shoe in her teeth, then turned back, dropped the *chancla* in the dirt, and cocked her head at Yolanda.

"She's gone, girl."

Rosalind Franklin lowered her head, picked up the shoe, and continued down the trail, her steps a bit heavier.

Sonja and Ghita walked hand in hand down the trail, and Sonja leaned her head on Ghita's shoulder. Yolanda was glad to see Sonja and Ghita back together. Maybe now they could put everything behind them and all be friends.

When they made it to the river, it flowed fast and full. The water roared down the riverbed.

"It's too fast to cross," Sonja said.

"The bridge!" Hasik pointed. "There was a bridge not too far from here where we can cross."

As they made their way along the river toward the bridge, Yolanda hung back with Hasik. Out of the corner of her eye, she saw Hasik smile. He reached out a hand and found hers. She squeezed it back, a comforting warmth coming over her.

They crossed the rickety bridge one at a time as the water rushed below their feet. When she reached the other side, Hasik was waiting with an orange flower. He tucked it behind her ear.

"Mexican flame vine," he whispered.

Yolanda grinned.

❧

On the other side of the river, the tall, tall grass was gone. In its place were young, flimsy trees, a few meters apart, with tiny white blossoms adorning the branches. They dotted the landscape all the way toward home.

Hasik stepped closer, plucked a leaf, and twirled it between his fingers. "Pecan trees," he said. "Saplings."

The heaviness in Yolanda's chest lifted for a moment. and she smiled. A pecan orchard had emerged.

Wela was right. She was right about so many things.

Yolanda walked between the trees, a sense of peace settling inside her, and played Wela's words in her mind. She gazed around at the young orchard, brought back to life for the next generation.

Everything had been set right.

The heat pulsed overhead as they made their way through the young orchard toward home. Although the trip back was much faster without the grass and the wheelbarrow slowing their journey, Hasik and Yolanda were slow and cautious on their injured legs. Hand in hand they walked together, neither of them saying much at all, the silence comforting and reassuring.

Hours later, as the sun was setting on the horizon and the great white house with the wraparound porch came into view, Yolanda noticed the red-and-white flag in the window was missing.

"Dad!" Yolanda yelled.

Sonja glanced back and smiled.

They broke into a run.

Acknowledgments

Writing a book is hard. So many people were vital in making this happen and I'd like to thank them.

First I'd like to thank my agent, Kristy Hunter. Without your enthusiasm and passion, I don't know where I would be. You are an eternal optimist and the perfect counterpoint to my tendency to be a bit of a cynic. You took a chance on me, and I am forever grateful for your support and kindness. I am so lucky to have you on my team, as well as everyone at the Knight Agency.

To my friends, early readers, consultants, and people who made this book better along the way: thank you so much for your support and insights. Sam Figiel, Paula Bowker, Sahar Davis, Marián Giráldez Elizo, and Georgina Kamsika. Tricia

Seabolt, my supportive and wonderful critique partner. Thank you for your invaluable insights—they truly helped get this project off the ground.

Thank you to my sister, Erin Weddington, whose input on everything, but specifically the Spanish, was vital. Any mistakes are my own, but without your help, I'd probably be on Google Translate making a lot more of them.

To my editor, Karen Wojtyla: thank you for helping me shape this book into what it looked like in my head. You have such a talent for raising questions and pointing out issues while letting me do the problem-solving on my own. Your feedback and passion for this project is felt. Thank you for taking a chance on me. I finally feel this book is at the place where I wanted it to be when I started.

Thank you to everyone at Margaret K. McElderry Books who believed in and helped shape and promote this book—Justin Chanda, Bridget Madsen, Elizabeth Blake-Linn, Penina Lopez, Tom Finnegan, and Audrey Gibbons. You all have done an outstanding job. Nicole Fiorica, thank you for all of your work on this project, constantly keeping me in the loop and sending me the best mail!

Victo Ngai, thank you for your absolutely stunning artwork for the cover. When I heard they picked you, I knew this book would be in excellent hands. Debra Sfetsios-Conover, it is obvious that the cover was designed with such a meticulous and thoughtful eye, from the spine to the tiny details on the back. You did an outstanding job. It takes my breath away every time I see it.

Bill Fogleman, who always had fierce belief in me, no matter what I wanted to do: it breaks my heart that you never got a chance to read this book, because I know you would have been so proud of it—and me. You have impacted me in so many wonderful and positive ways that I will carry with me for the rest of my life. Thank you. We miss you so much.

Thank you to all of my family near and far, the Weddingtons, the Figiels, the Acevedos. Every step of the way, I've felt supported and cheered on during this crazy publishing journey.

Thank you to my parents, Mom and Pa, for giving me the foundation and support to even think this crazy idea of writing a book was possible. And thank you for not getting too annoyed at me for reading thousands of books during dinner while ignoring the rest of the family.

Thank you to my daughters. It was the journey of motherhood that made me realize that I wanted to write, for real. It made me realize that if I could take care of two tiny humans, I might actually be able to start this writing thing. And thank you for napping so I had time to write.

And finally, thank you to my husband, Greg. Your constant support and love means everything to me. I'm so thankful that we found each other and have made this wonderful life together. I don't know how I got so lucky.